Stranded Princess

A TABOO ROMANCE

CANDY QUINN

PATHFORGERS PUBLISHING

Preface

Sign up to my newsletter to receive free, exclusive stories:
http://candyquinn.com/newsletter

Book Themes: Step-father/daughter, taboo, breeding, virgin, blowjob, exhibitionism, kink
Word Count: 38649

One

L eah's long, blonde hair trailed down her back as she looked at Monty as they waded in the pristine oasis. He was staring at her, again, but hoped she wasn't going to notice. Both of them were naked, their clothes having been stolen from them, and he could not stop looking at her large tits, her firm ass.

And she couldn't stop staring at him, either. His cock was substantial, bigger than she ever would have imagined, and his firm abs and strong biceps were so seductive.

She moved towards him, her arms wrapping around his neck in a hug, but a soft moan tickled his ear as her firm breasts pressed into his chest.

They'd escaped death, together, but there was no escaping what was to come. It was so wrong, so desperately wrong, but she wanted him all the same. He was over twice her age, but dashing, loving, and hung. She felt it as it twitched against her leg, and when her green eyes met his, her heart stopped for just a moment.

The one person in the world that she wasn't supposed to fall for.

And she was about to offer him her first time.

Two

Leah'd signed up for a job as a guard on an archaeological expedition to the remote regions of the world, off across oceans and desert. It wasn't for the pay however, or anything of her usual sort. This time Leah was in search of someone she'd lost long ago: her own father.

Or more precisely, her step-father.

Her mother had always told her he was dead, but at some point in recent years, her mother had accidentally blurted out the truth: he's alive out there, somewhere.

Getting the whole truth from her mother was impossible of course, but with some prying, persistence and a lot of screaming, she found out his full name. And the rest she put to her investigative skills.

He was a renowned archaeologist, researcher and adventurer. The dashing Montana Barnes had travelled the known world and beyond, had his works in every library across the world, and was something of a folk hero of sorts at that. One of the most famous novels of the day was inspired by his failed expedition to the southern seas, that instead had him finding the first clue to the lost Atlantans. His ship had crashed upon the rocky shoals, and he'd survived there with but a handful of crew for several years, before being rescued. And all the while he'd dug up, catalogued and prepared some of the most earth shattering findings in his field.

So when she found out he was preparing to head off on another expedition, she'd signed up. It was a tough competition for the spot, because most everyone wanted to work with the famous Dr. Montana Barnes: archaeologist, adventurer and rugged heart throb. But her skills were excellent, she had the training and experience, and won the position.

At first, she didn't say anything to him. She just watched, studied him. Though in reality it was a bit overwhelming at first. He was every bit the legend to behold: tall, dashing, ruggedly handsome, and he dressed both exquisitely and sparingly, showing off a hardened, toned body that was well used to hardship on the journey.

Of course, part of her awe was undoubtedly the fact that this was the long lost father she'd yearned for. And there was such an intense familiarity in him. Her mother and him had parted at such a young age, but still she had such powerfully familiar memories of him, being so caring, kind, and spending so much time with her. So much of herself came from him and those early years they spent together, except he was bigger, more masculine, and with a wealth of more earthly experience.

He was firm but kind with everyone, always had a bright, warm smile when approached. And so in time she did just that. At first she just started chatting with him casually as they journeyed into the wilds. She would off-hand-edly probe about his life, his past. Asked if he recognized the name of her mother--without saying it was her mother--and found out he did, they were colleagues long ago. But he hadn't seen or heard from her in many years.

When she asked him if he had any children, he sincerely and sadly said, "Regrettably, no. I never did settle down long enough to make that happen, though for a brief while I did have a beautiful little girl. But she was taken from me. I fear the Barnes name might die with me... just not this expedition, because I'll have you watching over me," he said with a warm smile and a playful wink.

She became convinced he had no idea of what happened to that little girl, which she already had a strong suspicion of. Her mother's attempt to imply he knew where they were but didn't care had been laughably insin-cere. She knew her mother enough to know when she was lying for her own benefit.

But after weeks of travel, and having set up camp for a couple weeks more during the excavation, she decided to take her chance.

It was night time, and she handed off her watch duty to another guard. She was to head to bed and rest, but instead she saw the glow of lantern light through her father's tent flaps, and she headed that way.

He was up going over some of the findings of the day, dressed in a red, gold and black silk shirt and pants. They were beautifully inlaid in the style of the locals, so much more beautiful than the clothes of all the other crew, who were largely sticking to frumpy work clothes.

"Oh hey, how can I help you, Leah?" he asked, a smile

on his face as he turned back to his table, brushing some dust and grime from a stone tablet.

She braced herself, having practiced it all for some time. She broached the subject of that little girl with delicacy, but he was distracted with work and didn't seem to put it together. So she brought up her mother, Lynn, and he gave her a placating smile, not putting all the pieces together yet. Her mother had changed their name when he had 'died', after all, so that he could never find them.

But when she asked, "Do you remember your and Lynn's daughter... Leah?" she saw the way the gears in his head turned. The realization dawning in his emerald eyes. He'd seen her papers when she applied after all, had hired her based on them, her references and her display of skill.

So he knew how old she was, he knew how the timeline matched up. And he dropped his tools.

"We were together briefly," he said, his voice soft and vacant compared to usual. "It wasn't much to dwell on, but..." he paused, eying her up and down. "She just vanished one day with you... I... I had no idea," he remarked.

And even without her skills of lie-detection, the teary-eyed expression of joy on his face as he saw her in a new life, making sense of the similarities in her and the girl he remembered... it was undeniable.

And they embraced, as father and daughter. A tight hug.

"I can't believe it," he said to her, clutching her tight, their eyes shut.

And then, in the midst of their special moment, oblivious to all that was happening outside... the dark figures slipped their fluted-instrument through the tent flap. And it was Leah who first went limp from the dart, held up by her father's arms.

He thought she had fainted at first, from the intensity of the moment. But when he looked down at her, he soon realized her eyes were open and she was paralyzed by some agent. The realization didn't come soon enough though, because before he could act, he too was hit... and father and daughter went down together...

Three

Leah had no idea how long she'd been unconscious. But she knew after the paralysis dart had hit her, the dark figures had swept in, and dabbed their mouths with some poisonous concoction that put them into a slumber.

When she awoke, her limbs were tingling, but they were working. The place was bright, the sun scorching hot, and beneath them there was only sand. They had travelled some distance from their excavation site, she realized.

And shortly after that, she realized she was naked. Stripped of everything and left out in the sun next to some other bodies.

"Bring the next sacrifices," came a croaking, horrible voice, and she saw--or rather felt, as she shut her eyes and feigned unconsciousness--as they came and took away some of the people at her side. Two more of her companions taken.

"Save those two for last," said the voice, before they shuffled off. "I have something special in mind, for Dr.

Barnes," he remarked with an ominous chuckle as he receded into the distance.

And when she dared to open her eyes, she peered over to see her own father, laying there, emerald eyes meeting her own green pair, his long ponytail down his back as he lay on his stomach.

"You okay?" he asked, in a very quiet, low voice.

She nodded, then dared to look up just a bit.

She saw they were at the foot of some altar in the desert, and at the top a great brazier burned, as black-cloaked figures loomed around it. She couldn't see the scene, but she heard the scream as some of her former companions were horribly mutilated and murdered.

She looked to her father, and he said, "We have to make our escape."

He slowly got up, his toned, muscular form completely bare too, and Leah felt a flush warm her cheeks as her gaze went lower. His large manhood was exposed, and even in such a state, he was an adonis!

There's never a time or a place to see your father in such a state, and perhaps it was the shock of being captured after such a tender moment, but it took her a few seconds to tear her gaze away from his nude body.

"Right," she said, pushing herself to stand, her motions slow as to not draw the eye of their captors. She didn't bother telling him. He was a master explorer, and that was kiddie shit.

She glanced back at him before she could stop herself, seeing his body glisten in the heat of the burning sun. It was a distraction, to say the least. Maybe it was just the adrenaline and fear being confused for arousal, but it was still a discomforting sensation.

So instead, she slowly began peering around for an opening for their escape.

The two of them crouched behind an old, weathered pillar, looking around. The dais where the cultists loomed was large, and too high to see the top clearly, except for the licking flames of braziers, and some more weathered columns. It sat in the middle of the desert, seemingly nowhere, with sand dunes stretching on into the distance until it reached hills and distant mountains beyond.

The cultists weren't keeping a firm watch, probably because they assumed the poison had done its job, and they wouldn't be waking up any time soon. But they had no way of knowing that her father and her were especially hearty, and resistant to such things.

A way to escape was tough to discern however, because there wasn't a lot of cover to hide behind on the escape. But then she saw it... some dunes had formed a trench, and if they stuck low they could probably avoid detection for quite some time. She looked back to her father to tell him, and found his emerald eyes upon her, lingering, slow to snap back up to her own gaze.

She swore the sight of his exposed member between those splayed thighs had swollen ever so slightly. But he ran a hand back over his long hair, his muscles glistening in the heat, his skin sun-kissed.

"We could start taking them out one by one, stealthily," he offered up, seemingly having his own idea. "I could use that ritual pike there, with the skulls, as a weapon. I'm good with a spear or lance," he said, his voice quiet. He didn't whisper, like an amateur, he just spoke lowly so the sound wouldn't carry.

She smirked at him, pleasantly amused. Of course he wasn't the type of man who'd simply try to escape. It always had to be an adventure, something daring and deadly and exciting.

But she took after her mother in that regard. The only good risk was a calculated one.

"Take the pike, and keep it in case they give chase as we move through the trench," she countered.

She pointed to the dune trench, and he noted it.

"Good eye," he said, for it was hard to see. In the glare of the desert heat, it was nearly impossible to place. He gestured to her to wait a moment, then he crept forward. He looked up to the top of the dais, then moved for the ritual pike.

There was a moment of intense tension, but he gripped it with both of his hands, and his glistening hard muscles bulged. He wrenched it free from its spot, then stepped back behind a pillar. He took off some of the extraneous skulls, leaving just the sharp tip. He tested its strength then nodded to her.

"Let's go," he said, and the two of them began to creep forward around the altar. He led the way, and she got a good view of her own father's round, firm backside, and dangling manhood as he kept watch for any of the robed cultists.

Her heart raced in her chest and she had to shield her eyes slightly just to force herself to look away. It was inappropriate to say the least, and yet... so tempting. She shook her head, trying to chase the thoughts away and focus on what was important: survival.

But, still... it was a tempting way to keep her moving forward.

They crawled along through the sand for some time. It left a trail, but she'd been wary enough to hide the beginning of the trail with some careful motions, before they vanished into the trench. After what seemed like hours, but must've been closer to fifteen, twenty minutes... she heard cries.

"I will not have that deplorable Dr. Barnes getting away... again! Find him!" carried that familiar voice she'd heard before upon awakening.

Her father peered back, twisting his powerful, gleaming body about in such a sensual manner.

"They know we're missing," he said. "Keep our heads down for now."

And they continued on, but soon... the frantic cries were followed by screams of terror. And she felt a tremble in the sand beneath them. Some of the sand from the top of the two dunes that hid them began to spill down into the trench, and both father and daughter tensed up, feeling something that was... off.

"Shit," he said, and the sand began to pour down, filling the trench as the quaking grew worse and worse. They had to climb up out of the trench, or risk getting buried alive.

Leah was suddenly half-buried in sand, and her father reached back, his strong hand gripping her.

"Here," he said, taking hold of her arm and pulling her

up out of the sand. They would be exposed, but they had no choice left.

But the moment they arose out of the sand, she looked back to see how close their former captors were, and...

What she saw instead, was something out of a story.

A gaping maw had opened in the desert, a black pit from which a giant, worm-like beast of pure obsidian arose. its jaws opened wide, and great writhing tendrils squirmed out. It's cry was like no animal of this world, and both of them had to shield their ears as some of the black robed cultists were snagged up by those tentacle-like appendages.

It was only by instinct that her cries were silenced by the pure shock of the sight, and though she stared in horror, she didn't move or make a peep. Some deeper part of her mind was activated to keep her safe, but nothing could save her from the sight of something that shouldn't exist.

What she saw, shouldn't be... couldn't be. Yet it was. And it broke her mind a bit. But then she felt her father's arm around her, and he was tugging her back away from the sight of it. And she realized he'd been talking to her a while.

"Don't look at it! C'mon," he hiss-shouted at her, as he forced her gaze away to meet his. And his handsome, chiseled face. It helped bring her back to reality, and together they got to their feet and began to run from the site of the eldritch ritual with as much speed as possible, abandoning all pretense of secrecy.

She feared that secrets could not be kept from that monstrosity. As if it could see beyond normal sight, feel beyond normal feeling. Maybe it was just her terror, telling her ghost stories as they ran, but she just felt as if that thing knew things beyond reason or logic. How could anyone hope to hide from that for long? Fleeing was the only thing to do.

But with her father gripping her hand, keeping her from giving into that inexplicable temptation to look back... she ran on. The two of them running ceaselessly, without stopping, without slowing, for hours on end, the desert sun beating down upon them as they seemed to defy the limits of endurance put upon mortals.

Four

It seemed like their escape had taken forever, but yet time had lost meaning. Until her father stopped and pointed, his glistening chest heaving.

"There! Water," he said, and together they made way for a waterfall in the desert.

And once they got close, she saw that it dipped down into a lush river valley, where--in that tiny little gash in the earth--lush greenery and sparkling blue water chased away the grim, sun-scorched reality of the desert.

"This way," he said, as he found a ledge to climb down onto, making his way down the rock face like an expert climber. Only he had no gear, just his bare hands and a crude, ritual pike.

She was exhausted, her body aching in ways that she had no idea she could ache. She had always worked hard, taken her duties as a guard and an explorer seriously, and was as fit as a young woman could be. But every part of her was now tight and throbbing. It was only the promise of water, such a base need, that drove her on to ignore all the pangs, and she began following down after him, her motions much more cautious.

As she neared the bottom, he dug his pike into the soil, then opened his arms. He reached up and grasped her as soon as she was in reach, helping her to the ground, placing her down with care, despite the exhausting run, his heaving chest. He looked down at her, their bright, emerald eyes meeting as he held her by the waist in his two strong arms.

"We made it," he said after a long pause, their two bare forms pressing together.

She could feel the heat from his flesh, and her arms wrapped around him, tugging him in against her so tightly despite the fact that her arms felt like wet noodles. There was just something about escaping an eldritch death that made one crave something more earthly, and his body against hers was the best reminder that she was alive that she could imagine.

His strong, bulging arms wrapped around her in return. And for only the second time in many years, her father embraced her warmly, lovingly. He held her tight against his hard, sculpted body, cradling her beneath his chin as he kissed the top of her strawberry blonde head. It was such an intense moment, and it was only interrupted when she swore she felt his impressively sized cock throb against her.

He abruptly cleared his throat, and muttered, "We should drink."

She wasn't dumb to the ways of sex, though her experience was more theoretical than practical. But even still, feeling that twitch, then his want to pull away was enough to tell her that her intuition was right. He was getting hard from her embrace.

For some reason, the thought made her grin, and she held him even tighter.

"I'm just so happy we made it, dad," she breathed into his ear. "I don't ever want to let you go."

And with that, he was unable to tear away. She held him so tight, and his own willpower to preserve decency and move on was pushed aside. So instead of ending their embrace, he squeezed her tighter again, kissed her once more. And though all his willpower wasn't enough to make that member of his cease it's throbbing, its slow growth, they remained entangled.

"I'm so glad you made it... my little girl," he remarked, his gleaming body pressed to hers, her breasts mashed against his hard torso. "It would have been too cruel a fate to find you and lose you all in the same moment..."

She nuzzled into him, her head brushing against his as she purred with delight.

"We have so much we need to do together. So much for you to teach me. Like what the fuck that scary fucking worm was," she said with a voice that was both awed and terrified.

He gave a wry chuckle at that, but even the joke couldn't break the sexual tension between them. Their two stunning bodies pressed together so hard, his cock partially--and undeniably--hard now, pressed between their two forms awkwardly, so that she felt every throb of that large member that had, for some time, been in her own mother.

"I don't know what it was exactly... but I think it was one of the Elder Beings," he said, perhaps trying to distract from what was a rather inappropriate moment for them. "Beings that predate time itself... they must have been sacrificing us to try and summon it. But... as often happens, it wasn't easily reined."

"Do you have that in common with it?" she asked, her tone coy.

He tensed up for a moment, then gave a slightly nervous laugh before it melted away into warmth. He caressed her smooth back, kissed her hair again.

"I guess I do, that's true," he said, his muscles bulging against her. "I'm so glad you found me though... for more reasons than one. Because it's going to be tough going out here. I don't even know where we are... they took us far." But try as he did to divert the topic to serious matters, the pulse of his desire throbbed between them, and he held her tightly, inhaling her intoxicating scent. Something so primal about the two of them that called to each other.

"Oh, I bet you have a lot of reasons," she teased, not letting up. "This feels like a very elaborate setup to one of the great adventures of Montana Barnes and his glorious daughter. You save her from grave peril, and promise to always protect her, as long as..." she trailed off, curious as to how he'd finish that sentence for her.

"...As long as you remain mine," he said, his voice husky and light then, as if the words came unbidden. He kissed her forehead. And while he tried to be sweet and kindly, the raging fire in his veins continued to broil, filling his cock to its full heft, causing it to strain upwards, nudging against her two thighs. As if that thick organ craved its rightful place betwixt them.

She let out a laugh, though it wasn't malicious or even

particularly chiding. It was more... smug. As if he confirmed everything she was thinking -- hoping? -- he'd say.

"I'd believe you set this all up, except I can't imagine how you'd bribe a giant beast to do your bidding when you can't even plead with your own organ to behave," she growled in his ear, kissing him there with a tenderness that belied her chastisement.

She felt his powerful, muscular form tense up at her taunting, but he didn't break their embrace. He held her, caressed her once more after a delay.

"I'm... sorry," he said, his cheeks flushed with more than just the exertion of their run. "It's all this activity, the narrow escape from death... always does it to me," he said, trying to excuse the lewd throbbing of his cock against her. And it was true enough, perils and great physical activity tended to leave him aroused. But this? Nothing but desire for her could explain how ragingly hard that thick, throbbing cock was.

"Well, how about we go for a little swim and see if that cools you off," she said, pulling away just enough to glance down at his engorged member as it throbbed against her.

She was not the most experienced with sexual matters, but yet... she knew to look at it, that her father's shaft was not only quite large, it was perfectly formed. It was like the mould through which all men's cocks should be shaped, it was so perfectly thick, veiny, with the tip a deep, dark purple that was so well-shaped and rounded. Pre-cum stained the tip even as he peeled back from her.

"Gods, you're... you've certainly grown up," he said, as he began to turn away bashfully to head to the water.

This time she watched him openly, enjoying his own discomfort. It was such a strange, new feeling. It was power like she'd never experienced before, and she was greedy for more. Still, she was exhausted from the escape, and she quickly followed him to the water.

Her father went into the stream, his powerful calves and thick thighs slowly sinking into it. It didn't come up deep enough to fully hide his raging cock however, but he crouched down, and began to drink, splashing some cool water over his muscular form. But even that did nothing to reduce the view she got. Seeing him pour water over himself, watching it cascade across his form, was like a special treat. Something so sensual and erotic, that countless fangirls would've killed for the opportunity.

She followed in after him, not taking her eyes off his gorgeous form. It had been a strange flurry of emotions as she'd surreptitiously watched him at the beginning of their expedition. She'd found him maddeningly attractive since the beginning, but seeing and feeling his nude form was a different type of experience.

Before seeing him naked, she might have been able to temper it, to fall into a natural, comfortable rhythm with him as father and daughter. To find what they'd lost so long ago.

Now, she wondered just how easily she could tempt him into doing something deeply forbidden.

She didn't have to wonder too long though. Because as they stood in the stream, washing away the sweat and desert dust, replacing it with the gleam of water... his gaze eventually strayed back towards her. Scanning her from top to bottom again when he thought she couldn't see him.

"You look so much like your mother when I first met her, but far more beautiful... there's no doubt," he remarked upon being caught, as if his eyes lingering on her tits and vagina was all about confirming her lineage.

She raised her brow at him, her green eyes glittering with amusement as her hands went beneath her large, heavy breasts, lifting them towards him.

"Are you sure, dad? I mean, you really had a good vision of mom's breasts..." she paused, bouncing her breasts in her hands, staring at him intently.

His eyes went wide, and while his expression said he was aghast at the impropriety of it... the way he continued to stare at her tits while his cock throbbed, said otherwise. But eventually he shook his head, ran a hand back over his hair, untying his hair, letting it fall down around his shoulders.

"You're... you're incorrigible," he said, as if a chastisement. But it was weak at best.

"Ah, well, you know what they say about girls who didn't have a father's firm, guiding hand," she said, still squeezing her breasts and toying with herself a little. It just felt *good* after their escape from death to have her nipples stiffen and her thighs slicken and her heart race with desire. It felt like being alive.

His cock jumped up, actually making an audible little sound with the water as he stared at her toying with those luscious breasts. He licked his lips and swallowed, his neck bulging as he let the band for his hair slide up over his wrist.

"I wish I could have been there for you all these years," he said, before finally tearing his gaze away from her lewd display. But only after he'd seemed to drift towards her closer, as if drawn magnetically.

"Mother always said, spare the rod, spoil the child," Leah said, frowning thoughtfully as she looked down at his throbbing cock as it bobbed in the water. "I guess that's why I'm so spoiled."

His hand lifted, as if he was possessed. And then... within less than an inch of her breast, his fingers curled back, retracting. He had been so close to helping himself. But then he licked his lips, the conflict plain on his face.

"Was it always your intent to... to play with me like this?" he asked. But then his fingers began to extend again, and she felt those strong digits graze her smooth, glistening breast flesh ever so slightly.

Her eyes widened in shock and surprise, not at all expecting a man like him to be so easily swayed to something so depraved. But the smile that warped her features betrayed her own lusts. It took her a moment to parse his words as she took a step closer to him, forcing her tit into his hand.

"My intent was to see what kind of man my father was," she said, relinquishing her breast to him and letting her hand drop to the water, finding his own masculine flesh and being much less tentative about it. "It's not my fault I found him to be a wanton pervert."

There was just something about them both that called to each other, and even him--far older, more mature and world travelled--was caving to it as she taunted him. Made him feel that heavy, supple flesh swell between his digits, causing that iron-shod cock of his to jump in her tight grasp all over again.

"I swear," he said, his gaze moving from her breast to her eyes, "if I didn't see it so plainly... if the pieces didn't all add up... I'd swear you were some temptress sent to ruin me," he wet his lips and squeezed her breast with a careful touch.

"Who says you're wrong?" she purred, and though she was toying with him, she was quickly finding herself out of her depths. She was still a virgin, and this was by far the furthest she'd ever gone in exploring her body with anyone else. But she didn't want him to think she was just a dumb girl, so she didn't let the act go. "Other than being sent, that is. I did send myself, much to mother's endless frustration."

"You're far more beautiful than she ever was," he blurted out, his hand caressing her smooth breast flesh, fondling it with unmasked desire. "Though... just as headstrong," he said, his cock pulsing wildly in her dainty hand, until she noticed the sticky feeling of pre-cum upon her wrist.

His other hand came up, then found its resting place upon her hip, just beneath her waist.

She let out a laugh, her strawberry blonde hair tickling down her back as she moved in even closer to him, so that she could feel his cock throb against her hip as she held him in place.

"Seems like you were the one I got my dark side from though, huh daddy?" she taunted him, the cool water such a relief against her aching limbs. Though as her arousal amped up, it dimmed the pain, giving her a slight reprieve from it that only made her desire more.

She felt his response to that word--'daddy'--in the form of a stiff twitch. But finally, he seemed to see how wrong it all was, and mustered the willpower to act, because his hand left her sumptuous breast and instead rose up to cup her cheek.

But though she felt for a moment that he might pull away, instead he leaned down, and his plush lips found hers. At first it was just a chaste little kiss, but then she felt his tongue slide along the seam of her lips.

It made her moan, and even she wasn't sure if that was a part of the act. Truthfully, she was acting over the top, but that was just her cocky way of protecting herself from vulnerability. She was taunting him for wanting her, yet she was the one who spent the last few hours fantasizing about what he'd look like as he moved atop her.

The kiss languished on, and then she felt his other hand touch upon her other hip. And together, both of his palms slid down around to her round, bubbly ass, fingers sinking into it, gripping it firmly. He then lifted her up, his powerful arms--despite the long run and exhaustion-- finding little trouble holding her up as her legs wrapped around his waist.

The kiss broke.

"I helped raise you, Leah. I'm practically your father..." he said, shaking his head a little, his eyes shutting. Guilt in his voice even as his dick jabbed up against her womanhood.

"It's only fitting that you're the one that teaches me to be a woman, then," she cooed into his ear. "I know it's what you want, and you can feel me. See how much I want it too." She could barely believe the filth coming from her mouth, but that pulsing between her thighs wouldn't let her be chaste, not then.

He moaned aloud at her taunting, sensual words, which

were far beyond her experience. But his hand reached in, fingertips sliding down between her cheeks, then finding the overly slick slit, coated in incestuous honey, making his dick throb and his whole body shiver.

"Teach you to be a woman...?" he repeated, the meaning of her words slow to sink in, since she seemed like such a practiced seductress, a sensual whore rather than a virginal girl. But he was kissing across her cheek, then down her neck as his fingertips teased her clit, and his cock pulsated next to it.

"Don't tell me that'd be a problem for you, daddy," she crooned, but she could already tell that his experienced fingers were quickly going to rob her of her wit and pomp. She started to moan beyond her control, her breasts pressed against his collarbone as he held her in his arms. "Come on, I almost died without ever knowing what a man's dick could do to me. Why shouldn't it be you? I'm yours, aren't I? You made me who I am."

"Fuck," he swore, her crass words unravelling every shred of willpower he managed to conjure up. And his fingers--teasing at her clit--froze up. She feared for a moment she went too far, but then she felt him aligning their bodies. That thick, incestuous cock prodding against her puffy folds.

"You're a gift from the heavens..." he moaned out, kissing her neck, suckling it a little as the bulbous crown of his manhood began to stretch her little slit open wide. He was being gentle... or perhaps just still battling with himself, and it was more like teasing than deflowering her, as he edged that thick dick into her a bit, then tugged back a little.

She was so wet that even the water couldn't wash away her honey, and she felt his crown press against her innocent pussy. She should have felt shame, disgust, something... but instead she pressed her mouth against his throat, kissing him and tasting the clean sweat that clung to his skin.

Her heart was racing, her body overheated, and her puffy slit kissed her father's dick with such need.

"There's no going back now," she whispered in his ear. "Might as well go all the way. It's the Barnes way."

He shuddered at her words, then bit her neck just a bit. As if trying to quiet his moan, but it didn't work. He gripped her tightly in his two arms, as he stood in the stream, holding her body up out of the water. And then... he pushed her down around his cock with one forceful motion.

All her cockiness, all her taunting and teasing, and she got what she wanted... her poor little virginal slit strained to its utmost limits, the soft pink turned almost red from the act. And he moaned out loudly, eyes rolling back into his head as his dick throbbed and pulsated inside her pussy.

She cried out, her head lashing back, her long hair spilling down over her ass as her own father took her innocence from her. It was exquisite, and her pussy squeezed his forbidden cock as he defiled her.

"Show me what it's really like, daddy. Don't hold back. Fuck your little girl," she hissed, clinging to him so tightly.

Forbidden lust, the thrill of having survived deadly peril, the body pumping full of hormones... it all worked together for the most insatiable need to rut. And her father gripped her ass and hips tightly, using her whole body like a fuck doll. He lifted her up, then crashed her down in time with his own hammering hip-thrusts.

He was unrestrained with his own moans and pants, filling their little grotto with such pleasured cries as he pounded into her at a faster and faster pace. He made those heavy tits of hers jiggle at first, then bounce, his stiff cock holding her in place with his ravenously raw motions.

He finally found a way to shut her up, to stop her incessant teasing of him. Instead, moans and screams spilled from her lips with no concern about who or what might hear. In that moment, she was finally free, filled with life and vigor and need. He had awakened a part of her that had been slumbering deep in the recesses of her mind, and the intensity of their sinful act reverted her back to her most primal self.

Her father--a man more perfect than she could've dreamed him up--was holding her, caring for her... guiding her into womanhood. And gods, it felt fucking great!

That rock hard cock that her mom had once ridden, was now pistoning into her with wild abandon. His heavy balls slapping to her ass, as he grunted and moaned. The water of the stream sloshed at his thighs as he pounded her pussy again and again, and a shudder trailed down his spine, filling his whole body.

"Mmmm fuck! My little girl," he panted out.

It was innocence and filth combined, and she held him tight as he made her ride him. It was easier than she expected, owing to his own strength and prowess.

"You like it?" she panted out, trying to pull away just enough so that she could see his face. She wanted to know that he would never look at another woman after having her.

He had such a strong jaw, his facial features chiseled and masculine. But then and there, with her pussy wrapped around his dick... he looked like he was brought to heel by the sheer, overwhelming pleasure of it. The satisfaction written on his face was unmistakable, and he had to struggle to keep his eyes open to meet her gaze for a moment as he nodded. Huffing and panting he spoke:

"You're so perfect," he grunted out. "You were made for me... made for my cock," he said, diving in and kissing her lips for a brief, but passionate moment before amping up his pace even more.

She kissed him back, letting him guide her in the dance of their tongues before he pulled back and let her look down between them. To see her pussy lips spread, tightly clinging to his hard dick as he took his own daughter. That sight was what tipped her over the edge, made her experience something she never had before.

Her cunny gushed honey over him as her muscles spasmed, her entire body seeming to sing to the heavens above.

He pressed his head alongside hers, cheek to cheek, watching the lewd sight of father and daughter joined at the loins. But as she cried out and came upon his cock, he felt a grin spread across his face. As if in victory.

"That's it... that's my girl," he cooed to her, keeping up his unrelenting pace, pounding into her as his own dick swelled up. "You'll never cum so hard as you do upon your father's cock, dear Leah," he huffed out.

Any sensible girl would have thought that a heinous

thing to say, but Leah's pussy only began to milk him more. His lewd words were music to her ears, and she wasn't going to hide it from him. She loved every filthy declaration that passed his lips, and aftershocks of pleasure shot through her.

In the height of their passionate tryst, his apprehensiveness, his guilt, had finally dissolved entirely. And she was left instead with the true, love-affair Monty: cocky, self-assured of his exquisite prowess. And he pounded into her with the expertise of a man who'd made love to many, many women.

But his arrogance was short lived, because that tight clench of his daughter's pussy was taking a toll unlike any other woman's. And he quaked, his balls tightened. And he kissed her, but without his usual finesse.

"L-Leah... g-gods!" he gasped, before slamming her down upon his cock a final time, and letting his virile cock erupt, shooting thick strands of his seed into her depths as he roared out into the once untainted grotto.

It was exceptionally careless, cumming in her like that. But it barely seemed to matter as she quivered against him, her pussy drawing up every ounce deeper into herself. It was so wrong, yet that got both of them even hotter, and she was grinding against him with such desire that he didn't even have a moment to consider his reckless actions. Instead, he just focused on how she cried out as he thrust so deep into her, her body arching and presenting for him.

He didn't pull out in any last ditch effort to spare her the risk of carrying her own father's child. He didn't apologize. He kept his dick within her deep, unloading all he had, and with the last of his wherewithal he lunged for her presented breasts, and found one, taking her nipple into his mouth as he suckled it in the final throes of his climax. Savoring yet another delight his daughter's body had to offer.

She squealed in shock, her nipple instantly stiffening against his tongue, her hand going to the back of his head and pressing him into the soft, large flesh of her bosom. She was a temptress, the way she so desperately wanted to share her body with the one man who should never taste of it.

He suckled and held on, accepting her open invite to ravish and enjoy her breast. And he kept at it, even as her world seemed to spin. It took a while to realize it was spinning because he carried her to the shore again, and laid her out on the sand beneath him.

Their loins were still tightly entangled, and his dick spurt it's last as he lay atop her. His tongue swirling around her teat, pulling at her sensitive nub as his breathing slowly began to stabilize.

She mewled and writhed beneath him, her strong legs still wrapped around him as she relaxed beneath him. Exhaustion was starting to set in, now that the orgasms had subsided, but she was still luxuriating in the taboo pleasures of his immaculate form.

They lay there like that for such a long time, the sun setting overheard. The only change was when he switched to her other breast, renewing his suckling appreciation for her endowment, until both were left tingling and aching from his enjoyment of them. It was only when his cock finally softened after the sun went down, that he slipped out of her, then pulled back off her breast to roll to his side next to her.

She curled towards him, her hand resting on his hip as she looked at him in the dim moonlight, a twinkle in her vibrant, green eyes. She didn't say anything. She just leaned in, giving him a soft kiss before she settled down to sleep after the longest and most exciting day she'd ever had.

Five

It was perhaps the most restful night's sleep that Leah had experienced. Though how much of it was the raunchy but satisfying sex with her own father, and how much of it was the raw exhaustion of narrowly escaping a grisly death--then fucking afterwards--she couldn't say.

She awoke to the sounds of life around her, birds chirping and singing, the babble of the stream. She rolled over to curl into her father but... found nothing.

As her eyes opened, she saw that there was no sign of him. He was gone. The bright light of the early morning left no mysteries, as she sat up and looked around. He wasn't anywhere to be seen about her!

Then, at that moment, she heard a sudden thump to her side, and sprang up reflexively! Only to see it was some sort of thick fruit from the tree above.

"You're awake!" came her father's familiar voice, as some more fruit fell down beside the other. "I was getting us some breakfast," he said.

Her eyes moved upwards, to see the sight of her naked father climbing down the tree. That man had a knack for climbing like no other, it seemed. And he was down to the ground in no time, landing on his feet with a bright smile, that wavered only slightly as he looked her over.

"I hope you feel nice and rested. We'll have to be at our best to survive what's to come," he said, brushing his hands together.

Even though last night they'd done something so taboo and foul, in the glittering sun of a new day, he still looked immaculately perfect. Those gleaming muscles so refined, his every aspect seemingly flawless to his style of dashing masculinity.

She could tell he was being careful to be as normal as possible, which Leah found both off-putting and endearing.

"You act like you've done this before," she said, putting a finger to her lips in thought. "Ah right, your shipwreck. So I suppose this is old hat to you now?"

He chuckled at her response, then plucked up the pike they'd taken from the cultists. He took it and then crouched down to gather up the fruit, his manhood dangling lewdly as he began to work.

"It's just another adventure! Except this time, I have my very own daughter with me," he began to slice into the fruit's shell-like exterior. "Very exciting," he said with a playful wink to her before cracking through the tough exterior, then peeling away a hole. "Here. The contents are drinkable. Then we can eat the flesh of the fruit inside."

"Sounds right up your alley," she said, grabbing the offered fruit and taking a drink of the nectar. "This is all new to me, though. Any idea where they dropped us off? I guess there's not much use trying to head back to camp, considering everyone was likely captured, and it's probably been raided by now."

He repeated the process on his own, crouching down and then beginning to drink from the fruit, before quickly finishing it off.

"We'd need to have some idea of where camp was before considering that. And right now, all I can tell you is that it's probably somewhere... that way?" he pointed off across the stream in a general direction, then gave a shrug, before slicing open the fruit entirely, to get at the juicy innards better. He did this for her as well.

"Oh! I have good news for you though," he said with a grin. "I found some supple trees when I first woke up and looked around. Looked perfect for a make-shift bow. You remember how to do that like I taught you?" he asked.

She watched him with just as much fascination as she did the first time she saw him as an adult, as if she could understand him through sight alone. Waiting for him to reveal his secrets with a subtle gesture or motion.

"I can fashion a bow, yes. It's important in the wilderness to know how to fashion all sorts of tools," she said, repeating something he'd told her as a child.

His expression blossomed, a bright, warm grin at her that spoke of pride. He laid down his pike with the dagger-like tip next to her.

"I put the wood there, with some other pieces I thought would make good arrows. Also found some reeds that might make a decent string, but... might have to sacrifice my hair tie for that," he remarked with a chuckle.

He had such an easy charm about him, he must've been a master at defusing awkward situations with anyone else but her.

"Natural fibers work best," she said with a small smile. She was still feeling so sore, but there was something endearing about him, it let her relax a little. That didn't change the fact that she knew how desperate he was to act like this was any other adventure, and how easily she could tease the devil out of him.

"Excellent. I can make a bow myself if I have to, but the spear is where I excel. So that'll improve our odds," he remarked, wiping away some of the fruit's juice from his chiseled jaw then smiling to her. "We should get to work on that stuff as soon as we can... we can last here a while if we have to, but... I'd rather get to work on getting out. While you do that I'm gonna try and weave a crude bag to carry some more of this fruit. Looks like we'll have more desert to trek through, after all."

She let out a soft groan at that. She rather preferred the little oasis, and forgetting that they were trapped in the middle of the desert with little idea of which way to head or what dangers lay ahead. It was much better to simply tease, rut, and sleep.

But instead she stood, finishing off her fruit and going to the wood, beginning the careful work of crafting something with enough power behind it to be helpful.

It took them both a while, especially since the only sharp instrument they had was the jagged occultist blade. But eventually, they both finished their respective projects, she had a working bow, and some sharpened wooden arrows, and her father had fashioned a crude satchel, enough to carry a big bundle of the fruit he'd gathered.

"If we had time, I'd say some clothes would be a nice next step, but..." he trailed off, his eyes unwillingly glancing over her form as he stood up, grasping his pike in one hand.

"But we are just so pressed for time in this desert oasis, and really can't dally around here to make clothes. I get it," she smirked at him. "Still, we're likely to get burned if we don't find something for the hottest points of the day."

She swore she detected a hint of flush to his cheeks there, and he cleared his throat.

"Well... I mean, we can always stay the day and take time to fashion some crude garments... if you think that's best," he said. He reached his free hand up to scratch at his thick, lustrous ruddy-blonde hair.

"I don't think it'd hurt to make the most of our time in relative peace while we determine the best way forward. I know that you're a swashbuckling adventurer that gets off," she paused deliberately, "on taking unnecessary risks," she paused again. "But there are times when caution is warranted."

He froze at that remark, his cheeks flushed. He looked away, then lowered his satchel of fruit down to the ground.

"Y-yeah, you're right," he said, clearing his throat again, then looking to her. He was so handsome and self-assured usually, but she had a way of cracking his barriers. Making him awkward, like nobody else could. "I'm... about that," he said, stepping closer to her, tentatively. "I'm... sorry about that, last night. I... I shouldn't have done... well... any of that. But... especially not... inside... you..." he remarked so awkwardly. "I'll... I'll be better in the future. I owe you better than what you've gotten, as your father."

She waited for his sincere apology before she cracked up laughing.

"Yes, well. A girl grows up and has her father taken away from her for no reason, she gets some daddy issues, and all she wants is to please him. So maybe I got exactly what I wanted and deserved."

Her first words, about growing up without a father, it left a definite sadness on his handsome features. Regret, was the more apt term. He truly wished he had been able to stay with her all those years ago. But he reached out to touch her shoulder in a most chaste, paternal manner.

"No fault rests with you for anything, my dear daughter. I... I just want to do better by you. I got carried away, it's no excuse, but..." he ran out of words. Probably because he was making excuses even as he said it's no excuse.

"I don't think most men would get carried away by cumming in their daughter's pussy, but what do I know?" she grinned, moving towards him. "Regret doesn't suit a swashbuckler."

Again, he was taken aback by her brazen lewdness, seeing her step up so close to him. His eyes were wide as he stared down at her, his hand still on her shoulder.

"I... you're right on that last part. Well, all of it," he conceded. "Regret isn't something I've known in my life... until you came back into my life, and I regretted not seeing my little girl grow up," he said, then tentatively wetted his full, kissable lips. "So... you're... really not mad at me?" he asked, sounding both confused and surprised.

Her brows furrowed at him, her confusion matching his.

"Why would I be mad at you? I asked for it, didn't I?"

His confusion still didn't dissipate. It only seemed to intensify.

"Yes, I mean... aggressively so, but..." he raised his arm to rub the back of his neck, the act making his thick bicep and forearm bulge. "It was wrong and reckless and... you're my daughter, you have no responsibility for it. It was all on me to be the mature and responsible one. And I failed you there... epically."

"Failed in some ways, huge success in others," she shrugged, causing her buxom breasts to jiggle. "What's it matter anyways? Firstly, not like anyone knows, considering we're literally in the middle of nowhere, secondly, who gives a shit? I couldn't have asked for a better first time."

And there, finally, she cracked his facade of responsibility once more. A slight grin tugged at his lips, which he hurriedly tried to push back down. He squeezed her shoulder again.

"It was... I don't know that I should admit it, but... it was the most thrilling sex I've ever had in my life. And that... my dear daughter, is saying something," he confessed with a grin, before a tinge of guilt plucked at him again. "I shouldn't have confessed that."

"You shouldn't have, only because I'm going to remind you of it anytime you piss me off," she grinned. "So what, the off limits is tempting, dad. It's the way of the world. We might die out here anyways, might as well have some fun before we do."

He listened, his mouth opening as if to object partway

through, but he pondered her words, then said, "I won't let you die out here. I promise you that, but... you're right. Whatever happens out here is between us, and nobody else. We'll do what it takes to survive. And thrive. And... should you, uh... y'know, be pregnant... I have some skill with that sort of thing. I twice had to deliver a baby on an expedition, you know."

She laughed again, genuinely amused.

"Good to know," she teased, before leaning in and kissing him on his mouth. "I don't mind that you're a pervert. It just means that I can learn a lot from you."

He still looked surprised by that kiss, but a smile blossomed on his face again and he rubbed her arm, kissing her back.

"I'm... not quite the pervert you might think me as. I mean... this is new to me, at least. Or... what we did last night was, I mean. Not to imply we have to keep doing... it..." he remarked, then cleared his throat.

He had the look of such a fearless stud, but her words brought him down to the level of a near stammering teen again. He cursed himself for that.

"You've just discovered that the girl you raised wants your cock and that gets you harder than ever. You are a huge pervert, you just didn't know it until I showed up. Your other skills, though," she said, trailing her index finger down the middle of his toned chest, "I'm sure they translate to your new perversion."

His eyes widened at her crass words, but she felt the sensation of his hard cock pulsating against her, as close as she was. That thick shaft had risen up, and was prodding against her smooth flesh again.

"Gods... who taught you to talk like this?" he asked, in that fatherly way. But what wasn't fatherly was the way his hand trailed from her arm, down to her hip... then back around to her bubbly round ass. "I don't remember you always being this way, Leah."

"Well yea, we left before I hit puberty. Mom called me incorrigible a lot when I was a teen," she said with a shrug. "But I guess you've been too busy living your adventures to read all the tales written about them, huh?"

He looked both flabbergasted and impressed, but he gave her a smile.

"You're a truly unique young woman, my lovely daughter," he remarked with a fond compliment, trying to sound sweet, even as his cock was still throbbing against her. "I guess... it's pretty nice we get this time alone to get to know each other at last."

"This time alone with your thick shaft desperate to be buried in me again as you tell me all about how you want to make me yours for all time?" she asked, pressing her hip in against his hard-on. "You know, some of those books about you were very detailed, but the real thing still puts them to shame."

For a moment he was aghast, but then...

"You mean that?" he asked, looking pleased. "I mean... I know some of those tales were bawdy and sensational but... you really think I outdo 'em?" he asked with a grin.

"You literally saved us from an unbelievable monster without even pausing, then you ravished the beautiful young maiden in a desert oasis. If anyone wrote that down, it'd be seen as too fanciful to be believed," she said, kissing his neck so gently. "Especially if they wrote about how that hot young maiden with the huge tits and toned ass was begging for it and calling him daddy, especially since, yea, he's the only man who ever helped raise her."

His arms coiled around her, wrapping her up in his thick, muscular grasp. He held her, caressed her, both her thick, sumptuous behind, and her stunning figure. He inhaled her feminine scent, so alluring and primal, with no clothes on, and the desert heat to stoke her aroma. It only made his dick harder against her.

"She would be unbelievably hot for a tale such as that, you're right..." he remarked with a cheeky grin, kissing her head, then letting his hand stray from her side to cup the edge of her breast.

She leaned in, whispering in his ear, "But the thing is, daddy darling, that you have to feel a little ashamed of what you did. Because that just makes it hotter when you give in and do it again. That remorse, that regret, that shame is what makes it so delicious."

He tensed up throughout his body, but most of all in his loins. Where that thick, virile organ throbbed against her with such incessant need and desire. And though he'd frozen for a moment, he squeezed her breast once more after.

"Gods, you'll be the ruin of me, Leah..." he groaned, his thumb skirting the edge of her nipple, trading around her pink areola. "We should really... go... hunt, make some clothes..." he said.

"At this point, your senses for hunting are dulled, and in all the stories, one thing remained consistent. You were always at your best after bedding some damsel," she murred. "Unless you want to be responsible and take care of yourself while I watch."

He gripped her ass and breast tighter at those words, his cock leaking pre-cum onto her flesh. He groaned, grinding against her without even thinking of it.

"I can't trust myself to pull out of your pussy right now..." he confessed, his voice so heavily laden with lust. "You keep provoking my desires to levels I've not felt since... since ever. No matter how guilty and ashamed I feel about it," he said, his thumb pinching her nipple against his index finger.

She let out a soft moan of pleasure, licking the cusp of his ear. "You are such a dirty old man," she teased, her body shifting slightly to exert some pressure against his member. "You want your little girl to beg for it? Is that it?"

He kissed her again, his fingers sinking into the supple flesh of her ass, fondling her, teasing that breast as he ground his dick against her, smearing his pre-cum onto her flesh. He spoke in a deep, dark confessional stone, licking along her ear.

"Many other girls have..." he said. "They've begged me to debase and defile them. But you're so very special... far more beautiful and sensual than any of them... so perfectly shaped," he said with a groan. "How is it you're right about so much at your age?"

"I read a bunch of filthy stories about my father in doing research on who he was," she purred. "So in a way, you did help raise me into the woman I am today. Maybe I could have tempered my desires under normal circumstances. But these are not normal circumstances."

She'd managed to coax out the desire in him fully again,

so that all his pretense of being serious, of making preparations and getting ready to escape were forgotten. All he could do now was grope her, fondle her, grind on her and spurt pre-cum onto her smooth flesh.

"You felt the desire to be taken by me before you even found me?" he asked, curiosity, surprise and excitement in his voice as he slid his fingers in from her ass, to betwixt her thighs, to feel her bare, pink pussy.

She breathed softly against his ear, letting out a gentle moan as he touched her wet sex.

"I was attracted to a man that existed only on pages and in long lost memories. I never imagined you'd be better in person than I remembered. I don't know anyone who ever was better in reality than in fiction and childish nostalgia," she purred. Her arms went around his neck, pressing her breasts against his chest, her thighs parting for his hand.

He groaned lowly with such desire, his fingers curling in, teasing her slit, two of his digits spreading her labia open to slide inside. He slowly fingered her with the expertise of a man who knew a woman's body better than most men knew their own.

"How are you so fucking perfect?" he muttered amid his moan of desire, his cock pulsating wildly. He pulled his head back enough to look down at her, to admire her beautiful face, her buxom breasts pressed up into such thick mounds of cleavage.

"I take after my dad," she said, planting another soft kiss on his mouth. "Now, why don't you teach me something new before we have to leave our little paradise here?"

He stared into her glowing emerald eyes, so much like his own, and nodded to her, licking his lips with desire.

"Ever jerked a cock off before?" he asked, "Because you're right... I'm gonna be useless until I unload all this desire you pent up in me. And I know if I stick my dick in your tight little cunt I'm gonna do it as deep inside you as I can," he confessed, his voice dusky and laden with more desire the longer he spoke, making him sound as if he already regretted proposing something else.

"You really shouldn't want to knock your own daughter up so bad," she said as she let one hand drop from his neck, going between them and grabbing his shaft. "What would mother say if she knew, hm?"

As her delightful little hand found its way down to his cock, his eyes rolled back into his head as they fluttered shut, and he let loose a deep moan. That hard shaft pulsating in her grip. He kept his fingers lodged in her pussy, teasing her there as he shuddered.

"Fuck her... " he said with a hint of bitterness. "She kept my little girl away from me all these years," he nuzzled into her hair, before bringing his other hand down, gently peeling their bodies apart at an angle as he wrapped his digits around hers, to help guide her, beginning the motions of stroking his dick at a languid pace. "She had no right to do that. You were my little girl too."

"You claimed me with this," she said, looking at Monty's eyes and holding his gaze as she held his cock. "Is this what you had mom do? Get you ready for her?" she asked, curiosity edging in beneath her teasing words. "She never seemed all that interested in this sort of thing. I had to rebuy so many romance books when she tossed them."

He nodded to her words about how he'd claimed her with his cock, the same one she was then stroking with his tender guidance. That strong hand of his setting the pace and pressure, teaching her the exact right measure of how to squeeze his dick, which was much more than she would've anticipated.

"No," he answered her first question. "She wasn't much for foreplay... very... serious, even then," he said, swallowing as her smaller hand worked up and down his thick, veiny shaft. "It makes sense now I guess... she was always so... so work focussed. And raising the perfect child was her work of the day, when she accosted me in the research lab that night... began undoing her top without a word..." he wet his lips and moaned.

Leah listened to him as her hand worked his shaft, learned how he liked to be touched with just as much of her mother's seriousness. But she enjoyed him and his body in a way she doubted her mother could.

"So you think she just wanted your aid in raising the perfect girl?"

He nodded to her question, moaning lowly.

"Yes... now I do. It had struck me so odd at the time... she'd never shown any interest in me or any man. And then..." he spurt some pre-cum onto her dainty fingers, "fuck..." he muttered. "She seduced me, and we fucked, but when I met you, that's when I fell in love. I stayed with her because of you. And when she disappeared, I kept looking, but she changed her name, moved cities, hid you from me."

His fingers continued their slow, sensual motions of teasing her pussy, as he slowly took his other hand away from hers, to watch her stroke his cock on her own.

She kept his pace and desired pressure as he did, wanting to please him with her attentiveness.

"Maybe that's why she and I never got along. I always held it against her that she got rid of my daddy, told me he was dead. I had too much of you in me for her liking." She laughed abruptly at that, only losing her tempo for a moment. "Now I've had even more of you in me."

He grinned at her words and moaned, a low chuckle escaping his lips as he reached his now freed hand up to cup her cheek, caress it and pull her face towards him as he kissed the corner of her lips sweetly.

"You're doing such a great job stroking my cock, sweetie," he moaned to her, watching as his thick, veiny organ pulsated in her grasp. "Now that you've tried it... how do you like jerking a man off?" he asked in a devilish manner.

She grinned at him in return. "Oh, I haven't jerked you *off* yet, I'm pretty sure," she purred. "But I'm enjoying the jerking part. Though it does bring up a certain temptation."

He gave her that cocky half-grin of his as his dick throbbed and leaked even more pre onto her fingers. He kissed her temple then murmured into her ear.

"And what temptation is that?" he asked with a moan. "As you noted... it's not quite 'off' yet... there's still time..." he said deviously.

"Oh, no, dear father. It's the temptation to pull away and see the look on your face as I do so," she grinned wickedly, licking her lips. "I just think that would be delicious."

He grinned at that, then caressed her cheek before his hand slid to her shoulder. He put pressure upon her there, to push and guide her down to her knees.

"Here, let me show you the best vantage point for

seeing your father's face as you jerk him off," he said, his voice so growly with lust.

She pouted at him a little, but she did go to her knees before him, looking up at his face before then turning her attention to his masculine form. It was very different from seeing him in a standing position, and it allowed her to study him in a new way, to study his cock more closely.

His hand had slid from her pussy in the process, of course, but he brought those glistening fingers up to his face, inhaling her scent as he watched her.

"Mmm, there you go. Isn't that much better than walking away?" he said with a sigh, his free hand on her shoulder still, grasping it firmly as he licked his digits, then moaned, then followed it up by suckling at them. "Gods you taste divine..."

"I don't know if it's better," she said, tilting her head to watch her hand grasping his flesh, the way he throbbed against her fingers. "I'll let you know when I try it out."

His hand slid from her shoulder to her cheek, his thumb caressing her there as he looked down at her from above. The looming pillar of his throbbing cock obscuring their view of each other, but it was a beautiful juxtaposition.

"Mmm, this isn't a time for walking away... I need to see my seed splattered over your face. Deny me that and I have no idea what I might do," he growled, giving his fingers a final lick before smiling down at her.

She smiled back at him, pumping his cock with a slightly increased rhythm. It was different, from below, her hand curled in another way, but she still kept up the same motions as he showed her.

"Maybe we'll find out later what you'll do," she teased.

"Good girl," he said with a sigh, his broad shoulders relaxing a little as he savored her motions, the touch of her soft, dainty hand. He caressed her cheek, admired her beauty. "You are so marvelously beautiful... won't you play with a breast for me, dear daughter?" he asked as a grunt spilled from his lips. "I so loved it when you did that before..."

"Of course you did," she laughed, though she did dutifully start sliding a hand up along her torso before grabbing her tit and giving it a squeeze. "I can't believe the filth that comes from your mouth. Or that you'd be surprised at the filth that comes from mine."

He had to force his eyes to stay open, they so wanted to shut and enjoy the sensation of her hand on his cock. But he also craved to see her toy with her enormous breasts, see that flesh jiggle and move with her motions.

Standing over her like that, she got the full view of his torso, glistening with a thin sheen of perspiration in the morning sun. He was an adonis, like a statue of a god. And he was shuddering with the pleasure she brought him.

"Fuck," he grunted out, as more pre-cum spurted onto her fingers, his face contorted with pleasure in a way that made it almost look painful. "When... when the time comes," he started, as his heavy balls began to tighten, "I want you to aim it for your face... and tits. Got it?" he told her.

Her brows knit in thought, frowning in a serious manner before she nodded.

"Fine, but give me enough warning so I can close my eyes," she said definitively. "Is this a good speed?"

He nodded his head sharply, but then said, "A little faster," as he caressed her hair and cheek. That muscular hunk finding his shoulders hunching forward a bit, all his rippling muscular flesh tensing up, all those abs of his bulging out.

"Tell me something... something dirty, something secret between us," he said, his voice becoming strained as his cock swelled, his release getting closer.

It was a lot to ask in the heat of the moment as her pussy throbbed with need, and she bit down on her lower lip as she tried to think of something she hadn't yet told him. Well, something she hadn't yet told him and wanted him to know, at least.

She sped up her stroking before finally settling on a naughty tidbit.

"Well, the first time I fingered myself, it was while reading a book of your adventures," she grinned. "Never had much of an interest in that sort of thing prior to that. But then I remembered that the man on those pages was really familiar. I started to remember I knew you. And I couldn't resist."

His mountainous body quaked above her, glistening as his dick leaked even more pre-cum onto her hand.

"God that's perfect," he said, grunting. "It's... it's coming, almost there," he warned her. "Help daddy clear his head, you torturous vixen... fuck I'm losing my mind because of you," he said, running his free hand back over his ruddy-blonde hair, trembling with the intensity of his rising pleasure.

Her long lashes fluttered down over her brilliant green eyes, shielding them from what was to come. It made her a little sad to have to miss it, but she also didn't want to blind herself for their coming journey.

"I'd say you've lost your mind, dear father. You might as well enjoy it."

"I... I am," he confessed, before he tensed up, gave a choked moan and then... she felt his cock swell with the surge of cum. And a moment later, thick strands of pearly white cum were blasting over her face, coating her in her father's seed.

He was panting and moaning, gasping as he forced himself to watch the scene.

"T-tits, get the tits," he told her, ogling those gorgeous breasts of hers.

She tilted his cock down slightly, waiting to feel the spray against her skin. It was so warm as it began to slowly drip down her cheeks, over her lips, then across the breast she still held in her hand.

He greedily relished the sight of Leah holding his cock, and guiding it to plaster her face and tits in his creamy spunk. He twitched, his cock jerked, and the last few splatters of his cum landed upon those pillowy mounds, covering them in their pearly white.

It all felt rather intense, even if it was a way of trying to resist knocking up his girl... but he relished it, moaning lewdly as the last of his spunk drooled out onto her breasts.

"Fuck, oh fuck yes... even more gorgeous now," he panted, grasping her by the back of her head and neck.

She poked her tongue out, licking around her lips and tasting his seed before she opened her eyes and looked up at him with all the lust and intensity imaginable.

"You like marking a girl as your own, even when she

already belongs to you, mmm?" she asked, sliding her hand along her breast, smearing his cum on her nipple.

He refused to look away, watching every moment of her toying with his cum and her breast, relishing it. Even spent as he was now, she made his dick ache and throb.

"I own you, I marked you... I want to do everything to you, my beautiful, twisted girl," he said, a smile on his face as his chest heaved, catching his breath after that climax, caressing her hair tenderly all the while.

He looked at her with such lust, but then as she teased him, she saw that twinge of guilt return now that his overwhelming desire for her was momentarily sated. He opened his mouth as if to say something about regret but then... the sound of stomping hooves broke up their moment.

Six

A giant, tusked boar charged at them, obviously having come for a drink at the river and finding them in its domain. Thankfully, Monty was quick as he pushed Leah back out of the way, and then tried to spring to safety himself in the opposite direction.

But try as he did, he only had time to do one well. And while Leah safely rolled away to safety, Monty found himself hit by the boar and knocked back. He'd managed to avoid the large, sharp tusks of the boar, but he still took a thudding blow to his thigh as he leapt back.

Suddenly they were embroiled in a harsh reality of their hideaway: they weren't the only ones who'd want to make use of that oasis in the desert.

Monty was a famed adventurer, and she knew he could handle himself. But as he got up, she could see the pain in him as he straightened his leg out, and worse: his pike was basically beneath the boar's hooves as it turned around and looked back at him.

So without weapons, and bearing a battered leg, Monty

faced down the beast in a nude, crouching fighting stance. It stomped it's hoof, then let loose a terrible cry as it got ready to charge again.

It came for her father, and he jumped out of the way. This time able to avoid its attack entirely. But the boar expected it this time, it seemed, as it was quickly turning to gouge him again.

Leah was busy rushing for her bow and arrows, as she saw her father throw himself over the boar. His nude body narrowly missing its tusked attack, though he did strike against the beast's backside, before rolling away to the ground again. He picked up a rock as she took aim, the boar looking at her then. But he threw that stone at the creature, causing it to turn at just the moment her arrow fired.

And it hit the beast in its hindquarters.

It huffed in pain, and then tried to charge for Monty again, but its speed was lessened, it's gait uneven. He was able to dodge it better this time, and the beast seemed to be having second thoughts, as she lined up a second shot and her father raced for his weapon. He grabbed it up as she fired a second arrow, hiding the boar and causing it to squeal out in unholy pain.

But as the two of them, now armed, sought to finish the beast, it found renewed speed and vigor in its panic and began to flee.

"C'mon! Let's get it. It'll feed us for days," Monty said, as he began to run after it, despite his own bruised thigh. And while she should've been able to finish off the boar with her next arrow, the stream was winding, and thickly overgrown with bushes, vines and trees as the boar ran off, and soon she'd lost any hope of hitting it from a distance.

And thus began a day long hunt for the boar.

She got to see her father in the thrill of the hunt, a grin on his face as he beckoned her on whenever she faltered. But as much as he genuinely relished their survival antics, she got the impression part of his relief was just that it was a distraction from his defilement of his own daughter.

But after many long hours, they tracked the boar down to a little dead-end, and it turned to face them.

A boar didn't quite match up to the tales of his previous antics she'd read about, but this one was bigger than the two of them combined, and it was menacing, with a red light in its eyes. And together they took it on, with her pelting the beast with arrows, and her father showing off his own particular fighting style.

The glistening, nude man moved with grace and style, as he used his spear to jab at the beast, to keep it at bay and deflect its charges whenever it came for him or Leah. And finally, together, they fell the creature in the clearing, and her father raised his spear with a shout of victory, his torso spread wide as he grinned to her.

"The Barnes are victorious!" he shouted, before giving her a hard but chaste kiss on the forehead, then moving to the beast.

Before she could say anything more, he began the process of preparing the beast. He got her to start a fire, and in the waning light of day they prepared to feast. And all the while her father regaled her with tales of other such instances, or of how a flower he'd seen on their hunt for the boar would make a great seasoning, and got her to go get some.

By the time it was ready to eat, it was pitch black. The

only light was their fire, which her father was carefully tending to and feeding, to get the meat cooked just right. As an aside, he'd also begun to set up a second fire-pit, to smoke the remaining meat for longer keeping. He never seemed to cease.

But finally they sat, taking a load off and he had no more chores for her as they devoured their hard-earned meal by the fireside.

"You did great today," he said to her warmly, praising her work in the hunt. "And with some time, we'll craft some clothing to protect us from the desert heat, and smoke up a bunch of this meat. I should even be able to make drinking skins from the boar's hide, so we can cart water with us on the journey. It'll take a while, but... we'll be ready once it's time to leave," he said with a smile, trying to act the calm, caring father again. And not like the man who had shot his load over her face and tits that very morning.

"You mean, great today with the hand job, or...?" she asked, never willing to let him get distracted from the truth of the matter. Maybe that was her kink. Knowing that she could tempt him to do something so wrong, not just once, but twice.

Even though he'd prepared himself for her tricks, he was still taken aback by her comment. Perhaps it was just the warm glow of the fire light, but she swore his cheeks were red.

"On the hunt, and gathering the herbs, I mean," he said, looking away. "And, uh... as for the other thing. I'll... I'll handle myself from now on. And I'll keep you safe and protected too. We'll get out of this and get back to civilization, safe and secure," he remarked firmly. "That's my promise to you, sweet Leah," he said warmly.

"Pretty lousy promise," she said with a bratty sneer. "Come on, when I said you needed a little bit of shame to keep it hot, I didn't mean for you to turn celibate or something." Her brows were furrowed, and she was definitely not enjoying him trying to turn the tables on her.

He tried to continue eating, and being all natural. But he paused, then had to choke down his bite of boar. It took him a while to rebound, and they ate in silence until done.

"I'm gonna go clean up," he said to her, pointing to the nearby river. "Then we can turn in for the night. We have a lot to do tomorrow," he said with a bright smile, like the warm, loving father she had fleeting memories of from so long ago.

"You need your thigh looked at," she reminded him. Or maybe it was just an excuse. Either way, her tone was not one to be argued with. "I want to make sure it's not broken." She had little by way of medical training outside of some standard first aid, but she assumed she'd be able to figure it out once she was there. Just like she had with his cock.

But he ignored her again, turning and going to the oasis as he'd said, to clean up.

She followed after him towards the water, where the light was so much dimmer away from the fire. She came up behind him, as he crouched down by the water, washing himself. He didn't seem to hear her coming, as she caught him rubbing away more than just the bits of boar juice. His hands were rubbing lower once they were clean, and though she couldn't see clearly with the night time so dark, and his angle to her so poor, she had a feeling he was rubbing between his legs at that thick, heavy manhood of his.

That was not *fair!* He was cheating, and she did not like to be cheated. When she'd threatened to walk away from him and leave him wanting, he'd pushed her down so he could cum on her face and tits.

But she wasn't going to reward him for his arousal, either. So instead she noisily waded into the water, and began cleaning herself as well.

"Ulg, I think you got some cum in my hair this morning," she said, keeping a few feet away from him so that he could barely see her by the silvery light of the moon. But he knew she was there.

She heard him gasp and his hands move from his groin. His eyes moving over her, and while it was so dark, the moonlight bounced off the water and reflected onto her, helping him see her glistening silhouette.

"S-sorry," he muttered ashamedly. And he hung out, washing himself, and trying to wait her out, before it became apparent she was not going to leave him be. "We should head back by the fire and get some rest. It's late," he said to her, clearly hoping she'd go first.

"Yea, I just need a few. I don't have my usual products, so washing my hair is taking longer than usual," she said, arching her body. It let the moonlight caress her soft, tanned curves as she leaned back, thrusting her tits to the air as she wet her hair again. She rose up, shaking her head, making her breasts jiggle.

If he was going to try to play games with her, she was

going to win. He'd not get a moment's peace to take care of himself while she was left wanting.

He was stuck staring at her display, with his dick rock hard and untended to. He even risked reaching down to wrap his hand around his cock and give it a stroke as he watched at one point, but she caught it out of the corner of her eye and waded closer to him at that moment, making him dart his hand away.

And finally, after her merciless taunting and teasing, compounded by his total lack of privacy, he cleared his throat and said, "I'll meet you back by the fire..." the defeat ripe in his voice as he tried to go back and curl up, so he could at least hide the fact he was rock hard with arousal at the thought of her. A man's gotta save himself some dignity, after all.

"'Kay, I'll be right there," she said in a singsong tone, knowing precisely what she was doing to him. It was only fair, given that he was trying to deprive her of what she wanted. She didn't linger long in the water, finishing cleaning herself up in the stream before she returned to the fire, her body fresh and glistening in the warm light. "I figured before bed you could tell me a story about your adventures," she grinned as she joined his side at the fire. "I've missed out on so much, after all."

Monty had been laying there, looking like he was trying to drift off to sleep. But she knew better. She knew he was hoping she'd do the same, then fall asleep, and he'd have an opportunity to wake up and beat off. No, she wasn't going to allow that.

"Well... we really should get some sleep..." he began to protest, but the look she shot him silenced his argument.

And he cleared his throat, resigning himself to his fate. "Did you read about my time up in the mountains of Tibet?" he asked.

She had, but she wanted to hear it from him. Time was a tricky thing to track in the middle of miles and miles of desert and wilderness, but as the story went on, he started to drift off. She was adamant that she'd stay awake until he was asleep, every so often having to pinch herself as his soothing voice tried to lure her to slumber. She'd missed him so much in their time apart, and despite her forbidden desires for him, she really did feel like he was her home. The man who always made her feel safe.

So his story enraptured her, and she hung on every word until they finally slowed, and his breathing deepened and became more regular.

He'd lost the battle, and she needed to make sure he would also lose the war.

Seven

The next day, he didn't awaken with the same energy and capability that he had the previous day. In fact, she awoke first. It seemed he'd not had a good night's rest, because she saw him laying there, stiff as a log, arm covering his head from the light of day. It wasn't the swashbuckling adventurer from the previous morning.

But eventually he realized she was awake, and they both got up. He set about trying to care for her, just as he promised. And he gathered some more fruit, albeit slower than the day before. And that became a side to the boar meat. Which he then spent the rest of the morning continuing to treat and tend, to get the smoking just right, so it'd be dry and keep well.

After that, came the worst task of all: finding enough of the fibrous reeds, to try and make some clothes for themselves.

"Go gather as many of them as you can find," he

instructed her, as he settled in to work the boar hide. "It's going to take some work to get this hide fit for storing water. Probably won't be done for a few days, using what we have available," he said, bathed in the hot sun, illuminating his hard, muscular body in a golden hue. But despite how hard he tried to stay focussed, serious, his eyes did want to wander over her badly.

"Ah, I got a bunch yesterday while I was out getting the herbs you asked for. They were pretty light, so I figured it would save us a trip. How's your thigh doing?" she asked, looking smug with herself for having thought ahead and depriving him of another moment's privacy.

She could see the tension in his jaw at that, and he wet his lips as he worked over the boar hide with his knife and some assortment of gathered items that made no sense to her. Rocks, what appeared to be mud or... clay, and some other things. But he was experienced with surviving in the wilds, so she assumed he knew what was what there.

"Still throbs. But I don't think it'll be a big deal," he said, before regretting his choice of words. She could see that thick, long dick of his twitch between his legs as it dangled there.

"Well, if you want me to take a look at it, let me know. I'm told I have healing hands," she said as she stood up, letting her perky tits bounce as she gave him a radiant smile. She went to grab her reeds, but she was never far from him. All day, whenever he thought he might have a chance to rub one out, there she was, appearing just at the worst time to ask a question or get some help.

It was late afternoon, and he finally thought she was

gone, down to the water to grab something, but before he could even grasp his aching member, he heard her voice.

"Dad, I need to measure you for your loincloth. Well... your Adam and Eve leaf more like."

He was doing his utmost best to be a good father, and not give in again. But it was true what he'd said: his time with her had been the most amazing sex of his life. And whenever he let himself think about it, his only regret was not doing it with her more. But he pushed it down, and rose up, heading towards her.

"Alright," he said, coming towards her more gruffly, not his usual self. All that pent up tension was taking a toll on his demeanor. But he knew getting some clothes on them was the most important thing to help that at the moment. Because seeing her amazing body revealed was making it near impossible to resist. His dick was left twitching every time he glimpsed her.

She had worked the reeds into something somewhat soft by rolling them in her hands and braiding them, and she'd fashioned a long strip that would serve as his 'belt'. She held it up to him with a bright smile, knowing precisely what she was doing to him, and relishing every moment of it knowing that, eventually, he would have to cave.

"Here, let me wrap this around your waist and see how it fits."

He heaved a deep sigh, his broad, rippling chest swelling up before he let it out and said, "okay."

But as resigned and grumpy as he was sounding, the look of that thick cock before her twitching eagerly, ready to rise up at a moment's notice to her needs... betrayed what was really going on internally.

"You've done a good job with the braiding," he said, sounding genuinely impressed as he studied her work. "You must've done this kinda thing before," he said.

"I used to practice making bracelets in the summer," she said as she brought the middle to his hip, guiding it along his stomach before frowning a little. "Ah, it's too short," she pouted. "I won't be able to tie it up. Here, hold the ends and I'll grab some more reeds to get an idea of how much longer it should be," she said, her words sounding so filthy as she relinquished the belt to him and turned her back, bending over at the waist and presenting her firm, round ass to him.

His knees quaked as they went weak, sizing up that gloriously perfect ass. So firm and yet supple to the touch, but so perfectly rounded and bubbly to see. It was increasingly sun-kissed as the days went by in the desert, and he found his dick rising up. And no force on earth could've willed it down as he bit his lower lip to stifle a wanton moan.

While he resisted the temptation to reach out and touch her ass, nothing changed the fact that when she turned back around, his hard, daddy dick was going to be raging at full mast. The glimpse of her puffy pink labia between her thighs below ensured that. Nothing looked more tantalizing and perfect than that little pussy after all.

She dropped the reeds once or twice, cursing as she glanced over her shoulder at him.

"Sorry for the wait, it's just so slippery, and I can't seem to get a grasp on it right now," she apologized before finally grabbing the reeds and bringing them over to him. Her emerald gaze went right to his cock.

"Oh right, you're trying to be good. Sorry. I won't be long sizing you up," she said with a smile.

Part of his brain had shut down as blood rushed to his thick, sizable manhood. And he didn't have much to say as he watched her taunt and tease him so effectively. He swallowed heavily, his throat bulging as he shuddered.

"I, uh... would appreciate that," he said, his rippling abs tensing up as he felt that compulsion to claim her, to bury his dick inside her balls deep. But he refused to give in, and looked away from her, up into the blue sky that loomed overhead.

But his cock never let him have any peace, throbbing, twitching, bobbing. Leaking glistening pre over his thick purple tip, the aroma of his musk filling her nostrils as he stood before her.

And despite what she said, she was being slow with her work, her fingers a little clumsy as they grazed his hip, letting him feel her soft skin caressing his. It felt like hours before she finally decided upon how much more she needed to add, and set it aside.

"While you're here, I'll get your help to size me up so I know how long my bands need to be," she said, offering him his 'belt'.

Monty had barely managed to keep himself from caving to his desire as she'd sized him. So standing there, holding up the braided belt, and glancing from her to it and back again, he froze up. He was terrified, but part of him--a big, big part of him--loved the thought. And he was nodding before he realized what he was doing.

"Alright," he said, licking his lips as his dick throbbed before him.

She smiled at the fact that he was giving in, her heart racing with excitement.

"What do you think, hips or tits first?" she asked, brushing her long, strawberry blonde hair off her breasts, her perky nipples stiff as she presented herself to him.

He watched her rise up, those breasts jiggling as she moved and offered her body up to him to size. He swallowed heavily, his dick raging with desire as it bobbed and throbbed. He began to reach for her breasts without even answering her. Those strong fingers of his gliding along her smooth, gleaming flesh, as he could barely keep from groping them before he began to wrap the cord around her.

"You're so busty..." he muttered aloud as he tried to gauge how much she'd need.

"Right? God, I can't imagine how huge they'll be if you knocked me up," she giggled, her hands pushing his away as she grabbed both her tits and lifted them up. "Measure beneath them. I want to make sure I have plenty of support so I'm not driving you mad all the time as you try to fight your desires."

Of course, what she said was at extreme odds with what he felt about it all. Because seeing her slender little fingers sink into her large, heavy breasts made him very nearly grab her and claim her then and there. But he did it, albeit with shaking hands. And his thumbs slid along the underside of her two perky, full breasts, feeling that smooth, supple young flesh.

"Yeah... imagine..." he muttered thoughtlessly, imagining his little girl swollen up with his child. How stunningly, achingly full those breasts would be. "You'd make such a beautiful mom..." he said, as if in a trance.

"Might have already knocked me up, you know. And you can't really knock a girl up twice at once. But if you want to resist, then I'll respect that," she said, looking down at his hands and how long the cord was. "Alright, think I know how much I need for that. Now I need you to measure from my nipples. I'll turn around so you're not tempted to suckle them."

His head roiled with what she said. Thoughts of her already being pregnant, of how... would it really be so bad if he fucked her again? She's possibly already carrying his child, right? So why not? But he fought it as best he could, as if in a daze as he stared at her back and stepped in closer. His dick finding that round swell of her ass, smearing his pre-cum onto her.

"Shit, sorry," he said, as he tried to keep a hold on the braided cord. "If... if you are pregnant already..." he began, but couldn't finish.

"Then you're holding off for nothing. Just making me think you have a fetish for denying yourself what you can easily take," she said with a shrug. "Maybe you want me to play hard to get," she posed to him as she lifted her arms, helping the braid find the centre of her breasts and rest along her nipples. "Don't tug it too tight unless you're in the mood to play," she instructed, "and tell me how much longer I need to braid it."

He did his best to try and stay focussed, but at that point in the day--after all her teasing, his pent up need only growing--his best was rather pathetic. He fumbled with the braided cord a few times, cursed and found himself gravitating towards her. Inhaling the scent from her lustrous strawberry-blonde hair.

"You know... anal is a great way to practice... safe sex," he muttered aloud, the words seemingly coming straight from his dick as it twitched excitedly, but he visibly winced at having said. "F-Fuck, never mind. Forget I said that," he said, swallowing down as his fingertips glided over her back, sending tingles down her spine.

"You're the one interested in safe sex all of a sudden, not me. And if you want to talk safe, you could just be a good daddy and eat me out. There's no way you'll knock me up like that," she said, shifting her ass away from his throbbing cock. "So how big is it? Don't keep me waiting."

He shuddered at that, then let the cord slide from her figure, holding it up and showing her where about the length was.

"Uh, right here," he said, licking his lips as his eyes trailed down her towards her pussy and ass. Would it be so bad? He thought. Eat her out? It's not like fucking her, he reasoned. There'd be no penetration, and she'd be safe. And after all, depriving himself didn't mean he had to torture her too, right?

It was the flimsiest of excuse making, but he stared down at her pussy as he muttered aloud, "I'll do it."

Her brows shot up and her grin grew, before it turned to a frown.

"Aw fuck, I'm sorry dad. I'm incorrigible, just like mom said. I should respect your wishes," she said, wrapping her arms around him in a hug. "You're such a good man. These are just really weird times, and I shouldn't tease you like this."

The feeling of her body pressing to his, he couldn't help

it... not only was his cock raging hard, throbbing against her, spurting pre onto her stomach, but his strong, muscular arms went around her, grasping her firmly in an embrace. He shuddered at the sensations of it all, her touch, her scent... and aching to know what her taste was like.

"I..." he tried to speak, but he was so full of conflict, and couldn't formulate words that weren't awful. "I love you so much, Leah," was the best he could manage as he squeezed her tight, and struggled to keep his hands from sliding all the way down to squeeze and grope her ass. "I'd do anything for you..."

She kissed him on his jaw, and even though she was pleading a good girl case, his cock was still trapped between their flesh, and she was subtly grinding into it.

"I know, daddy. But I want to see how much you mean that," she purred before she pulled away, looking down at his hard, throbbing cock. "Maybe if I miss my period, you might change your mind about taking care of yourself. But until then, I'll help you keep your conscience clean."

He was ready to fall to his knees and beg her to let him eat her out. He was desperate for more of her touch, her contact, even if--short sightedly--it'd only damn him to being more pent up and in need, and willing to do whatever his lust bid. But in that moment, hearing her say that... he looked up to her face again, dumbfounded.

"Ah, uh... okay," he said, licking his lips again, feeling his heart thud in his chest so heavily. And his dick pulsating in time with it.

"Come on, I'll join you and braid up the rest of the bands while you work so you won't be lonely," she said, once more cutting off his chance at privacy. She wanted him to want her so bad that absolutely no force on earth would stop him, and at the rate he was going, he wasn't going to last the night.

W ork went slowly with her purposely teasing and distracting him, keeping him from clearing his head with some release. But she didn't really care. The beautiful desert oasis they'd found themselves in was sizable, and lush. There was enough food and clean water for them to live indefinitely there without issue.

People would pay endless sums of money just to taste such a paradise, so why rush to leave it?

But as the day wore on, and it was time to get the fire started again, her father's distracted mood only grew worse. He cooked up some more boar meat, and that was filling and delicious. But as night blanketed them entirely, and she kept fouling up his attempts for some privacy, it came time to sleep again.

Though judging by the wide-eyed look on her father's face as he lay there, staring up at the night sky, she knew it wouldn't come easily to him. Again.

"It's hard to sleep without the noise of others, huh?" she said, letting him know that she was awake as well. "Just you and me, alone in the world. Who knows when we'll hear the hustle and bustle of other people again. But getting used to the quiet of nature..." she trailed off.

He didn't have words with which to reply to her, he just grunted his agreement... or whatever it was, and continued staring off. And eventually, all her attempts to tease and prod him wore her out more than him, and she drifted off.

But she awoke later, hearing him. He was still wide awake, and even without seeing him, she knew he was grasping his thick, raging hard cock, slowly stroking it in an attempt to get himself off without her realizing and waking up.

"What was that?" she asked with a start, as if she'd heard another boar or wild animal approaching them.

She felt him tense up beside her, his hand slowly drifting from his cock.

"Just me," he said, his voice gruff and low, from the lack of sleep, the masculine desire that was polluting his mind, keeping him from being able to think like a person.

She relaxed, taking in a deep breath.

"Shit, that scared me," she said, letting out a little laugh and moving closer to him so that she could rest her hand on his chest. "Fuck, your heart is racing too. Here, feel mine," she said, grabbing his hand and pressing it between her heavy breasts. "I thought some wild animal was going to come and impale me. I'm glad it's just you."

She could see his gleaming emerald eyes in the light of the dying fire. Then felt his hand as it did more than just feel her heartbeat.

Those greedy fingers wandered over her breast, squeezing and groping at her soft yet supple flesh, and his lips leaned in for hers. That desire in him no longer able to be bottled and kept in check as he tried to make out with her wordlessly.

Her nipples stiffened against his hand and she let out a little moan against his mouth, squirming beside him before she pulled her face back a bit.

"Are you going to impale me, daddy? Because I want you to either take what's yours or go to sleep," she purred in his ear, her tongue tracing along the cusp of it.

Again, he didn't speak, but he nuzzled to her face, his lips moving from hers to kiss at her jawline, to her neck. He moved over her abruptly, his much taller, stronger body pinning her beneath him as she felt that nervously twitching cock, so eager for release.

"I can't... can't help myself," he groaned, nibbling her earlobe as he ground himself down on her, his hand squeezing and fondling her breast, feeling that flesh swell between his digits as he moaned and pinched her nipple between two of his fingers.

"I think you should be helping yourself to me as often as you want," she murmured to him, her excitement having woken her up completely. "You already claimed me as your own. You probably knocked me up. And still I'm here, begging for you to cum in me again. It really hurts my feelings when you say no," she pouted.

"I'm sorry," he muttered immediately, kissing her pouty lip as he let his strong, greedy hands grope and fondle wildly, growing more and more ravenous. He groaned and shuddered as he pushed her legs open wide, his dick throbbing wildly. "Daddy wants you so bad, all the time..." he confessed. "So bad it hurts," he rumbled as he pushed aside all last lingering remnants of his self-control.

"Nothing, nobody else but you will ever do again," he said, between smacks of their lips together.

"I'll hold you to that," she said, her fingers going to his hair, running through it. "But you were still a very bad daddy making me wait. So I have a deal for you and you're going to take it, and then tomorrow morning, we can get to living as man and wife, hm?" she asked.

He halted at her words, his body going stiff but for his hands and hips, that continued to grind his dick on her, to fondle her breasts. But otherwise, he stared into her eyes so still. His glimmering emerald gaze reflecting the moonlight and fire as he stared.

"Man and... man and wife?" he repeated dumbly, swallowing as he looked to her.

"Tomorrow. Tonight, you're going to show me you're sorry. You're going to eat me out and make me cum. After that, I'll let you jerk yourself off until you're ready to shoot your load in me, and then you're going to do it, nice and deep. And tomorrow morning, I'll be yours. Your little daughter-wife."

Had a shred of rational thought left in his head, he would've pulled away and told her that was too far. Beyond too far. That it was messed up and would ruin everything, her life, his reputation. Everything. And even more than that, it was just so deeply, deeply wrong... to not only fuck his own daughter, but to claim her as his bride? He should've recoiled in disgust and snapped to his senses.

Instead he nodded to her, eyes wide.

"I want to eat you out," he said, licking his lips and looking like he was famished with hunger. "You smell so... so delicious," he said, his voice taking on a rumbling, gravelly edge there as he nuzzled to her, his hand not on her breast sliding up her thigh.

"Mm, good. Don't touch yourself until I'm done. I want you to teach me how a master does it, and your attention has to be focused," she said, parting her legs more for him as her hand went to her other tit, squeezing it. "I've been pent up too, you know, and that wasn't my choice," she purred, lifting her hips towards him. "Being a good girl is highly overrated."

He watched her every motion, gripping her thigh as his gaze swept over her deliciously displayed body. He lowered his head, kissing down over her large breast as she held it, then across her taut tummy.

"You should get anything and everything you've ever wanted," he husked to her, as he grew closer to that intoxicating scent of her pussy. "I am so sorry for being such a bad man to you," he exclaimed, as he found himself kissing around her puffy, glistening slit.

True to her words, she was needy, her pussy so wet as she presented herself to him with such desire.

"I want you to spoil me and defile me. You can do that, right?" she asked. She wanted him so bad, and she had no scruples like he had. For her, this was the sexual awakening of a lifetime, and her youthful, smooth body was calling for his. They were made for each other, she was certain of that, and she wasn't interested in pretending they weren't.

He nodded his head without thinking of it, letting his full lips smack around her labia, as he drew inward with each new kiss. Until finally he kissed directly upon that glistening pink flower of her vagina.

"Anything... for you," he rumbled, his dick straining so hard as he caressed her smooth skin, then inhaled her scent deeply. Before finally licking at her slit, it sent a tremble through him as much as her, as he had his first, real, direct taste of her pussy. And he let loose a deep, desirous moan as that flavor of his own daughter drove him even wilder.

She moaned in time with him, that first feeling of a mouth on her pussy such an unexpected delight. It felt so primal and worshipful all at once, and it sent a shiver up her spine.

"I've been dreaming of fucking you for so long," she moaned. "I never thought I'd really get the chance. It was all just embarrassing fantasies, but it was the only thing I could ever get excited for."

His eyes shut tight as he tasted her pussy, heard her confession. He devoted himself to that glistening young slit he'd deflowered, licking it not only like a man ravenous with hunger, but with such utter devotion. He was without his morality, without his rational mind after her teasing, but one thing he did have... was his desire for her. His craving for her, and everything to do with her.

So the older man put himself to the task, grasping her two thighs, sinking his thumbs into her soft inner thigh flesh. He licked over her slit, swirling his tongue about her clit with each pass, growing more intense with each new plunge along her gash. And the only thing coming from his throat were not words, but deep, husky moans and groans as he swallowed her honeyed arousal.

It had been hell for her, teasing him. Pulling away and resisting him. Pushing him to his limits to see how long it would take before he would crack. She acted like it was nothing, but inside, an inferno raged, and she was so close to her own end before he'd hardly even began.

But her father's skill was impeccable, with this as in

almost all things. He lifted her thighs up to his shoulders, hooking them over him as he tongued her pussy deeper with each new pass of his wet muscle over her folds.

He rumbled and moaned, sending pleasing little humming vibrations through her clit as he paid her back for the suffering and longing she'd had to endure the last couple of days. And while his dick raged so fiery red, with such a desperate, urgent need to get relief... he kept committed to the task of pampering her young slit, of treating it to such a masterful eating out as he bathed her puffy, needy folds with such eager care.

It was a sensation like no other, and the orgasm that built within her was unique. It was slow, but the pressure it was building... She was almost afraid of how intense it was becoming, and she cringed away from it, trying to fight his grasp and avoid losing complete control to him.

But against her father's expert ministrations, she was just a novice. A beginner. She was at the mercy of his strong hands, his powerful body, as he kept her pinned there, kept up his assault with that lashing tongue over her sensitive pussy. He suckled at her clit a moment, drawing out that sensation as he buried his face in between her thighs and drank of her incestuous honey like it was life saving nectar.

She was fighting a losing battle, just like he was, and as that building pressure began to bubble over, she was completely taken off guard by just how strong the pleasure was. She was twitching on him, writhing, struggling, but he held her in place, making her feel those sensations as they crashed over her. And when finally that orgasmic release came, she screamed, her entire body alight with bliss.

The whole river valley and the desert beyond got to hear her scream her pleasure out into the night, as she lay there, bathed in the glow of the fire. Her father incessantly licking at her sensitive clit, driving her into deeper and deeper pleasure, the sensations more than she could tolerate.

He growled and gripped her flesh tighter, holding onto her and refusing to end his ravenous feast on her femininity, owning it, devouring it with that sense of possession. Longing. Need.

She had no thoughts left in her head. She was void of anything that wasn't ecstasy, her entire body softening to him as he laid claim to her once more. She lost count of the jerks and spasms of pleasure that he brought from her as honey gushed against his lips, but struggle as she may, he was going to make her feel every last pulse of orgasmic bliss as he could manage.

She'd had to wait a long time, endure a lot of torture in her own efforts to tease him. But it paid off, and then some. Her father's insistent tongue continuing to stoke such overwhelming sensations of pleasure in her body, the kind of climactic finish she didn't even imagine but a few days prior, when she was still a virgin.

And the beautiful sight of her powerful, broad-shouldered father hoisting up her lower body, to get at it deeper with his tongue, to let that muscle slide into her folds and taste her reservoir deeply, added to the moment. Her dad was such a stunningly masculine figure, gleaming in the fire light as he pushed her beyond her limits.

She was drunk on her lust for him, completely weak and stolen of all energy and words. She was just a pleasured husk, writhing and moaning as he took what he wanted from her body, and gave her everything she never even knew she needed.

She was too weak to struggle any longer, and so she lay there, watching him through lidded eyes, a dumb grin on her lips.

She'd done it. Like all girls dream of, she had her daddy wrapped around her little finger. She just had to go about it a bit differently from most. So she got to watch as her father continued to tongue and lick at her pussy, unrelenting as his dick throbbed in the air, and he seemed intent on eating her out throughout the entire night, he was so addicted to her taste, her tight little pussy leaking it's exquisite flavor onto his tongue.

He had brought her beyond pleasure, to a place where there was just nothing but the two of them and the intense sensations that he was making her feel. She was losing her mind, but had never felt better, and she let out another low moan.

"Your turn," she managed.

He was slow to register her words, and lift his head from between her legs. He was breathing heavily as he brought a hand up, wiping some of the glistening juices from his jaw, licking away the rest from around his lips.

He lowered her thighs down, keeping them spread widely as he loomed over her, taking his hard cock in his hand. But then, in his lust-laden haze, he began to guide it towards her puffy pussy, ready to take it. And she realized his head had been emptied of everything but desire and had to put a hand at his groin, just above his dick to stop him from pushing it right in.

She wanted it so bad, but she had to teach him a lesson, and letting him sink in wouldn't do it. It was torture for her, but she had to keep him for herself. To make him never want to resist her again.

"Jerk it. Then cum in me when you're ready to pop," she murmured, watching him through her heavy eyes.

His eyes snapped to hers again, as she reminded him of the deal. And while he was disappointed, he had no room to express it. He was just too damn desperate for her. And so his eyes looked back down to her pussy longingly... as he began to pump that thick, veiny shaft.

He'd been seeking a moment to beat off for over a full day, but there he was at last, given permission to do so by her. And she got to enjoy the view of his rippling hard torso gleaming with a thin sheen of perspiration as he stroked that long girth, his moans and grunts filling the air as precum spurt onto her body.

She watched him with such fascination, even in the haze of her post orgasmic arousal. He was so hard, so thick, and she wanted so badly to feel him take her. But tomorrow morning, she'd get that. For the night, she'd just get the satisfaction of having him wrapped around her finger.

"A big load for your little girl, daddy?"

"Y-yes," he grunted out, as she could see the glistening head of his cock in the light of night, clear as day. That massive manhood pumping up and down over her as it leaked more pre onto her body. "S-so much... I need to blow it all deep inside you," he said with a moan. "It... it won't be the same if I can't unload in your pussy," he insisted, lust clearly driving the man and not his brain. "I don't know why I ever thought jerking off alone would help... nothing will help but your hot body," he declared with a long groan.

"That's right," she said, giving him a long, lust-filled smile. "You should use me as your little cumdump. It's the only way for you to keep your head about you and keep us safe out here," she purred, her hips wriggling beneath his cock. "And the thought of you breeding me, making me swell up, my tits get huge... Doesn't that make you hot, daddy? It makes me so hot."

He watched her, listened to every filthy, depraved thing she had to say... and nodded, as his fist beat up and down the length of his girth, his pants and moans filling the night air as he brought himself closer and closer to his own release.

"It makes me hornier than anything else ever has," he confessed as more pre spurt onto her puffy pussy lips. "I want to make my little girl into my breeding whore... I want to empty my every load into your pussy and knock you up for the rest of my days," he said with a shiver that travelled up and down his spine. "G-...getting close," he panted out.

"Don't you dare waste a drop," she warned, her hips lifting up, letting him grind against her pussy and her over-sensitive clit. It sent another rush through her, and she shuddered, moaning again. "I want to make sure that before we're rescued, that you knock me up, so you can never leave me again."

He pressed that tip to her folds, but didn't dare enter yet, as it wasn't quite time. He obeyed her, spoiled her, just as promised. He had that much wherewithal about him and no more. But the head of his cock did drift towards that entrance, nudging against it from time to time as he stroked his manhood up and down.

"I don't ever want to leave you," he said, his voice strained, as his heavy balls began to tighten beneath his body. "Don't let me be stupid again... carry my child baby, be daddy's girl forever," he said, his eyes glistening as he strained, his shoulders hunching. "You... you want daddy to knock you up, baby girl?" he asked, breathlessly.

"More than anything in the world," she moaned, the truth spilling out from her lips so easily. "I've never had fantasies about anyone but you. About making you mine forever."

It was all so twisted. To not only fuck her own dad, but to play these games. To risk--no beg for--him knocking her up, to make him jerk his dick off and only at the last moment cum inside her... it was messed up. Even by the standards of the stories she used to read. But seeing her father bent over her, his every sculpted muscle glistening in the moonlight, as he neared his release...

It all felt perfect. More than perfect.

"I'm... I'm gonna-- can I?!" he asked, begged, his dick twitching against her pussy, spurting more pre as he struggled to hold back at the finale.

"One thrust," she said, offering herself up to him and his hedonistic desires. "And tomorrow, I'll be your wife." She didn't know why the thought thrilled her as much as it did, but just being his, having him bound to her, obsessed with her, was the ultimate aphrodisiac.

And her father obeyed. Just in the knick of time. Because that thick, throbbing, veiny dick slammed up into her with one smooth, forceful motion, parting her labia, stretching her narrow little pussy canal around his raging, incestuous hard-on. And he threw back his head with a loud roar as he came hard.

The pretenses of trying to be a good father, of trying to restrain himself... were gone. And instead there was just the glorious sight of her father's body pressed tightly to hers, his dick vanishing up inside her and making her lower torso swell with his excessive girth. And inside her...?

She felt every pulse, every throb, as he shot out his pent up load. So much seed built up since that time he'd taught her to stroke him off. And now all of it was flooding her depths, feeding her womb what she craved, helping ensure that by the time they were out of here... she'd be carrying her father's child, and he'd be hers forever.

But in that moment, it was just so glorious to get what she wanted. To take his seed, after having seduced him and beaten down his morality, his reasoning.

He grunted, his dick twitched inside her, and his whole body was ripe with tensed, jutting muscles and veins as he seemed to cum and cum and cum, more of that virile seed flooding her with each moment.

She came with him, so sensitive from his tonguing that his cock slamming into her sent her over the edge again. Her pussy massaged him, milking him of every ounce as her hips lifted to him, making sure he was as deep inside her as he could manage. She was still so tight, and he was so huge, but she loved the ache of him pressing against her inner-most barrier.

His bulky, muscular torso fell down upon hers then. And together the two of them moaned and cried out in their long, intense climaxes. Her father's hard, glistening form tightly grasping her as he willed his seed to do its work and sew itself inside her, against all laws or morality.

That rich, husky voice right in her ear as he moaned and shuddered, until at last he was spent, and all he had to give was deep inside her. And those strong arms wrapped her up against him, and he showered her with sensual kisses on her neck, shoulder, ear and face.

"Don't pull out," she whispered in his ear. "I want to know you want it, even once the guilt comes. And I want you to know how much I want it, and for me, the guilt never comes. You're going to make me yours forever, right daddy?"

As his needs were finally met, some sliver of rationality and morality tried to seep back into his mind. But he wouldn't let it, not then. He was still drunk on her, and while he'd cum, he hadn't gotten everything he wanted. He hadnt' gotten to fuck and claim her as a man would. And so it was easier to nod to her, because that lust was still in the driving seat.

"Forever," he grunted out, his dick twitching inside her. His lips kissing her neck, suckling her earlobe as he groaned. "You're my beautiful, perfect daughter-wife..." he husked in appreciation.

"And tomorrow morning, when you wake up with that hard cock, you're going to bury it within me, and make it official, right? Without me having to tease you?" she asked, her pussy gripping his cock possessively.

He nodded his head firmly again, his dick still lodged deep within her, as rigid as ever, sealing in his seed, locking it into her depths to do its work.

"I'll be good to you, I swear," he said, kissing his way towards her lips. "I'll use you as my sweet, little cumdump forever," he pledged, his will driven by pure desire and nothing else. Desire for the most beautiful girl he'd ever met. His own daughter.

Eight

L eah had her father wrapped around her little finger. She'd seen his guilt and reluctance, and also his yearning for her, and she'd played it to the limit. So that even when he awoke the next morning, pangs of guilt lacing his conscience... his rock hard, morning wood was still in charge.

And in the bright sun of the early morning desert, he cozied up against her by the ashes that were their late night fire. And even as she still slept, he put his hand upon her hip, and nudged his thick cock against her backside.

He was finally able to relieve his pent up burden the night before, but not fully. Not completely the way he needed. He needed to take his little girl properly, not just jerking off until the very end to feel her tight, warm pussy around him. He needed more of that little slit of hers, and he grasped her thick ass cheek, parting it from the other to expose her slit as he began to prod at it with his needy dick, glistening at the tip with pre.

She was still slick from the night before, or maybe even

a pleasant dream she was having, and he glided across her slit. She was puffy from their rutting, and her pussy looked so pretty as it parted along his shaft. A low moan came from Leah's lips, but she still seemed to be mostly asleep.

He was ravenous, and though he was still racked with guilt and feelings of failure, his need for her was overpowering. His pledge to her--even extracted in his most vulnerable moment of needing her so badly--lingering in his mind.

So he began to push his hips forward, that nude, powerful body of his sinking the tip of his cock into her, stretching that tight little puffy slit open wide around the head of his manhood as he moaned and shuddered.

"Oh gods," he quaked, feeling that wet slit engulf the sensitive tip of his manhood, as he lay on his side, cozied up against her in the bright sun.

It was the first time he took her because he wanted to, without her practically begging him. But all the same, she'd demanded it, and that helped ease his conscience. Just a little. Not enough to matter, but enough to let him push more of his length into his sleeping princess as she began to moan.

He groaned, biting his lower lip as he fed more and more of that thick, veiny dick up into her tight little canal. That needy shaft craving relief as always, craving the cling of a woman's pussy to milk it dry. But most of all... his daughter's pussy.

He'd foolishly pledged to be true to her, to claim her forever as his. But even as that guilt burned in his veins he just rocked his hips to pump his cock into her, trying to edge it in deeper with each moment, yearning for that sweet sensation of her young slit wrapped around his every inch.

She shifted, her legs parting and back arching towards him, and he could tell that she was coming to, but still groggy. Her moans were becoming more steady, and she was inviting him in, even as she was trapped betwixt sleep and wake.

It was so wrong, taking her like this, as she slumbered, even if she'd told him he had to. But that made it so exciting, so... delicious. He could use her however he wanted! The power he had in that moment over her body was intoxicating.

It made his dick swell to new limits, straining the walls of her slick little pussy canal. He grew more bold, shutting his eyes as he pumped his hips harder... faster. And then he let go of her bubbly round ass, sliding his hand up to her breast to cup and fondle it as he worked himself into her.

"Fuck... yes," he groaned out, as he reveled in the raw hedonism of it all. Claiming his daughter as he liked, even as she lay unconscious. It was wrong on so many levels, but that made his dick pulse faster, spurt some more pre into her nubile, fertile depths.

The sleepy moans of delight only egged him on further. Even as she slept, she was still so wet and willing for him, her recently deflowered pussy now shaped perfectly around his thick cock.

"Ohh," came a rumble of delight, Leah's heavy tit manipulated in his hand as her wetness grew around him.

He grew increasingly rough with her as his own lusts built, his dick fiery with need, throbbing wildly as he pumped into her, his groin smacking against her round ass with a loud slap. Those fingers sank into her breast, her nipple pinched between two of his digits as he grunted and moaned.

"My sweet... sweet daughter," he panted out, cock swelling. "My hot little daughter-wife," he said, remembering her words the night before as more pre shot out of his broad, purple crown, splattering against the entrance to her womb as he worked himself into a frenzy, focussed only on his own pleasure, on how good it would feel to cum deep inside her and knock his own daughter up.

She moaned again, her ass pressing into him, letting him dive deeper into her pussy. Her body was beginning to stiffen as she woke, giving her more control over her movements and letting her palm dig into the ground and keep herself from bucking forward as he thrust into her.

"Ohh, daddy," she murmured, her breathing quickening as he thrust into her. As she became more aware of what was happening, her pussy only slickened more, letting him fuck her even faster.

And he took full advantage of it. And soon, they were no longer on their sides, spooning together. Her father was top her, pushing her face down into the grassy mat that was their bed. Her one breast feeling the braids, the other still clasped tightly in his hand as he rut her with a ravenous, undying need.

"Baby girl..." he grunted, cock swelling and spurting some more as he shuddered all over and licked his lips. "F-fuck... I'm such a bad daddy," he lamented in a voice laced with moans and lust.

It was so animalistic, the way he was pinning her down, forcing his dick between her thick thighs. She pushed her ass towards him, and he thrust in deeper against her firm ass. The position was sending jolts through her, and she was moaning into the grass mat as her body tingled with pleasure.

"Good daddy," she corrected him.

She didn't feel the sting of guilt, of having done something wrong. And why should she? She was the daughter here, he was the parent. She was getting what she wanted, but he was the one with the responsibility to behave. No, she felt no guilt, just enjoyed the exquisite feeling of her father's thick, hard cock pumping into her hard and ravenously, making her ass ripple and her body quake.

"You want to be daddy's lil' pregnant slut, don't you?" he asked amid his pants and moans, his muscular body glistening in the early morning sun as he rut her so very hard and fast, his balls slapping against her mons as she pushed her ass up into him.

"More than anything," she moaned in return, her ass wriggling with excitement, even though she had to use so much energy to fight against his force and keep herself slightly aloft. It was a losing battle, but the longer she could get his dick thrusting in just at that right angle, the closer she got to her own orgasmic finale. "I know you want it too!"

"I do!" he admitted in the haze of lust as he hammered into her hard and fast in search of his own desperate release. Though he'd certainly never have confessed to that with a clear head. But it mattered not as he squeezed her breast, gripped the back of her neck and hammered into her.

"Fuck baby girl... daddy needs to cum inside you so badly," he growled out. "Need... need to make you my lil' breeding bitch," he grunted, his eyes rolling back into his head as his pleasure built.

All pretenses were lost, all guilt and shame burned away by the intensity of their lust, and for that one perfect moment, they were just raw and unbridled. It was perfection, and it was his words that sent her reeling over the edge of delicious insanity. Her pussy clenched around him, making it harder for him to pull back as her muscles began to spasm and massage his thick, throbbing cock.

She screamed, her entire body tensing and releasing with such intensity.

And any shred of decency in him that bid him to pull out of her, to not risk knocking his own daughter up again... was overwhelmed. By his desire, by the pleasure that intensely tight little pussy created in him. He gasped, his breathing ragged, his thrusts coming on haphazard and then...

He pounded down into her with such raw intensity, his dick shooting off thick strands of creamy white seed, flooding her depths as he quaked and moaned. He thrust that cock against her, letting her feel each pulse of his manhood as he sought to knock up his own daughter... and while the guilt began to seep back in even before he was finished, he didn't let reason and logic win out and cause him to pull back, he consummated his love for his daughter-wife, grunting and groaning as he squeezed her breast oh so tightly.

He might excuse it, later, by saying that she would have been mad if he'd pulled out, and he'd be right. But it wasn't that. It wasn't about what she wanted, or how she'd have been pissed off and deny him the tight clench of her pussy in revenge.

He came in her because he wanted it.

"Oh fuck, fuck, fuck!" she called out as she milked him of every ounce of his seed.

Oh, he definitely feared being deprived of that pussy ever again. He knew deep down, even if his logical mind denied it, that he would never be the same again after experiencing his daughter's tight little slit around his cock. What the hell else could ever compare? But in that moment, he pushed aside guilt and reason alike, and just reveled in how good it felt to claim her, mark her as his, and sew his seed in her womb. The wrongness made it better in that moment, as he spurt more seed until at last...

He sighed and fell down atop her, panting. His chest heaving as he left his dick embedded inside her deeply, his hot breath on the back of her ear as he pressed upon her body.

"Isn't it so much better when you misbehave?" she purred, her ass still wriggling against him, teasing him a little.

He groaned and moaned, his dick twitching inside her as she teased him with that thick behind of hers. But he licked his lips and squeezed her in his arms.

"I'm going to hell," he lamented in his deep, rumbly voice so tinged with need and desire.

"You'll have me for company," she giggled, one arm pushing underneath her as she tried to get a little more comfortable and look up at him.

But as she began to lift and turn, and he began to slowly, lazily shift with her, she saw the glinting tip of a bronze spear pointed right at her face. Then another, and another. All around them were the tips of glinting spears, as shadowed warriors ringed their position.

"You're too damn hot to resist anymore," Montana lamented, kissing the back of her neck, still unaware of the threat.

"Uh, dad... we have an audience."

He nuzzled into the back of her neck, kissing her still.

"Let the animals watch. I'm enjoying my sweet little daughter-wife. It's my honeymoon," he rumbled, as she saw the ominous figures brandishing those spear tips at them both.

She stayed still, not even wanting to elbow him and risk one of the warriors getting a little too excited about piercing them both.

"Dad, we're surrounded by a shit ton of guys with spears and they don't look friendly."

Her father stiffened--all over--and finally opened his eyes to find a spear tip nearly thrust into his eye.

"...Shit," he said, as they were both taken prisoner.

Nine

T he trek through the desert was rough, but at least they didn't have to spend it all running for their lives. Instead it was just while ringed by scantily armored guards, their brass armor covering little--just their heads, chests, loins and forearms--as they were taken back to wherever they were being brought.

Their hands were bound behind them as they walked side by side in the nude, his cum drooling down her inner thighs as Monty and Leah made their way. The guards hadn't even said anything yet, their intent unclear as they'd captured them.

"So uh... where are we headed?" Monty asked. "Not that I don't mind a nice trek, it's just nice to know your destination," he said. Then repeated it in another language she didn't know.

It only got a few odd looks from the men, but that was it.

"I don't suppose they speak Esperanto," Leah muttered, keeping close to her father. "At least they'll protect us from any charging boars or demonic worms, maybe. Or maybe they'll sacrifice us to them," she pouted. "Fuck, just when things were getting good, this had to happen."

He looked to her, his brow furrowed. He opened his mouth to reassure her, then was hit by a wave of guilt.

"Maybe this is my punishment for what I did..." he muttered lowly, as the guards kept them moving forward with the threat of those spears.

But now, at least, she could get a better look at them. And there was something distinctly... familiar about the way they dressed.

"Random guys aren't going to punish you for fucking me, and they're certainly not going to punish me for it. We were probably just on their land or something," she said, her eyes scanning the guards and trying to figure out where she recognized their armor from.

Her father opened his mouth to speak, but then a guard interrupted them. His voice was gruff and hard to understand, but she got the gist of it.

"You are being brought for your trial. For violating the sanctity of the Pharaoh's private grotto," said the guard, jabbing his spear forward. "Now keep moving ahead," he said with a glare.

"Yea, like I said, that was the Pharaoh's private grotto," Leah said to Monty. "But we didn't know that." She spoke up to the captors, and tried to explain, "Where we're from, every inch of land is marked if it belongs to someone, we didn't realize this was private property."

The guard glared at her, then raised the butt of his staff to hit her with it. But her father blocked the blow, taking it with his own side. He didn't make a sound however, her father just glared at the guard as they continued on.

"We'll plead our case in front of the Pharaoh then," Monty said, showing no weakness even as she knew that hit was gonna bruise.

She frowned at him, sympathetic, and bit her tongue about any snappy retorts and protests she wanted to make. It was a challenge, though, keeping her brattier nature in check. Still, she recognized that it was life or death they were looking at, and she hated to see her father hurt.

So as they walked, she simply kept close to him, trying not to draw any further attention or aggression in their direction.

The rest of the journey went without incident, as they stuck close together. And then they saw it... it didn't appear real at first, and they both thought the desert heat was clouding their minds.

Yet... there it was. A gleaming city of white, gold and intricate art woven in various colors of blue, green and red. It was nestled among some cliffs, hidden from view except by one angle of approach, but it was walled, and from behind the walls they could see obelisks rising up. It looked unreal. Like a place out of time.

And as they neared the front gates, they saw what appeared to be two sphinxes flanking the entryway.

"What the...?" Monty said, staring in awe and confusion.

Leah was just as taken aback. She didn't have the experience of Monty, but she'd been studying archeology and other cultures from before she could even speak, given the early influence of her father on her life. What stood before them was more fantastical than reality, and for a moment, she had to wonder if they were even still on planet Earth.

"How is this possible?" he muttered aloud. "It's like... we travelled back into time to ancient Egypt," he said in disbelief as the gates grew closer and closer, then swung open for their approaching party, to show the well cut roads of stone along a river that ran from a canyon further back amid the hills and cliffs, leading on up towards a pyramid-shaped palace.

Though Leah noticed that the people seemed subdued, or rather... morose. Many kneeling, a lot of dark colors worn, some sobbing.

It didn't exactly fill her with promise for the Pharaoh's goodwill and generosity to two interlopers who defiled the entirety of the private grotto.

"How much do you know about Egyptian Pharaohs?" Leah muttered to him, trying to keep her gaze slightly lowered. She figured it was better to err on the respectful side when one was marched through town, naked except for some rope, on the way to plead mercy.

"Well... a bit," her father said to her in hushed tones, the two of them behaving respectfully... or what they thought passed for respectfully. "The biggest thing I know, is that... they all died thousands of years ago," he said.

Though she noticed as she glanced to the guards, that they appeared almost as confused by the sight as she and her father did.

"I don't think everything is alright here," Leah murmured, gesturing towards the guards with her head. "I don't want to ask, but also... what the fuck?"

Her father looked to the guards cautiously, then back to her. His brow furrowed.

"It looks like the locals are in mourning," Monty said to her, as they continued to make their way towards that palace at the far end.

"Quiet!" ordered a guard, and they were brought to be silent again, until at last they were at the stairs that led up to the great palace. Another guard--or someone working in the palace at least--came rushing down, speaking to the man at the head of the guards.

They exchanged words for a while, and both Leah and Monty strained to hear them.

"--dead! He passed away last night from some mysterious ailment," they heard from the man who spoke to the guards.

"This is grave news," said the guard, before ushering the others to lead the two of them into the palace. "Let us complete our duties quickly," he said.

"It's never good when a trial runs quickly," Leah said quietly. "If you have a plan, now would be the time..."

Monty looked to her, then around at the guards. He seemed to take a moment to think as they climbed those polished white limestone stairs.

As they neared the top, he feigned a stumble. The guard behind him jabbed his spear towards her father, and in a move that was equal parts bold and insane, she watched as her father moved his hands behind him to cut the bindings on the tip of the spear.

It all happened so fast, but he grasped that spear shaft with his hands, then sliced the bindings open. And in a flash, her father spun around, spear in hands as he struck one guard in the face with the butt, then jabbed at another with the tip, not fast enough to hit him, but soon enough to drive him back.

Leah was astonished, her heart beating in her chest with excitement as she stuck close to Monty's side, lest someone try to grab her. She offered up her own bindings to him, for when there was a moment that he could free her, she wanted to be ready.

His quick motions were such a turn on, and she cursed the fact that they weren't in the grotto anymore, because Pharaoh or no, she would defile that place some more in that moment.

Instead though, her father did his best to push back the guards, make them retreat. And when one was foolish enough to attack, he deflected their spear and jabbed him in the shoulder, forcing him back, bleeding.

The guards were shocked by her father's prowess, and the two of them retreated up towards the top of the stairs. And as they did so, he saw her offered hands, and those bindings, and he moved the spear with precise motions and freed her as they reached the top.

It was then she saw a guard up there, pulling his bow from his back and drawing an arrow.

She had a good understanding of distance, velocity, arcing, and did the mental calculations. She pretended not to see the archer, and didn't make a move. The instant that arrow was sent flying, though, she pushed her father to the side as she ducked down out of the way, leaving it to whistle past her head.

The two of them were able to defy death once more, and the arrow sailed past them to the guards below, forcing them to duck and cower as well, since they weren't certain if it was arrant friendly fire or directed at them.

But together, father and daughter--both nude and glistening from the hot, desert sun--ran at the archer. The archer went for a sword at his waist, but her father knocked it from his hand, then struck him in the side of the heat, knocking him unconscious. And leaving his bow and arrows free for the taking as he spun around to take on the regrouping guards.

Her towering, sculpted father took them on with a flourish of skillful maneuvers that were dizzying to even watch. She almost felt sorry for them having to take her dear old dad on.

But not that sorry for them.

She grabbed the bow and arrows, and waited, watching for someone who might be getting a little too close, a little too adventurous. And the second she saw a cunning rogue sneaking in to try to take advantage of Monty, her arrow sailed through the sky to put an end to it.

Together they faced off against the armored guards, nothing but their spear, bow and arrows, their two nude bodies working in beautiful unison as they bested the guards again and again. But more were rushing from below to join the fray, so even as they defeated the guards who had captured them together, more were on their way.

"We have to get out of here!" her father said, and she knew it was true, but they were deep inside the town, and the stairs were the only way down. And they were currently being surmounted by reinforcements.

"Shit," he said, looking at Leah. "We have to head

inside," he said, as there was literally no other option as he turned to lead the charge.

She managed to fire off another arrow, taking down the first of the guards that swarmed up towards them, then turned to follow after Monty.

Together they entered into the most awe inspiring view they'd ever seen--well, except for each other's nude body-- and looked at the giant hall, with beams of light coming in from sources in the ceiling above. Great columns of marble or limestone adorned the halls, and a great throne was atop some stairs at the very back, made of gold and adorned with gemstones.

From along the halls more and more guards came, and they had no choice but to head up, and hope the banners behind it hid an escape.

They climbed the stairs, keeping the guards several steps behind, when they saw the truth: there was a way out behind the throne. As she tried the emergency exit, her father fended off the guards, avoiding any serious harm as he put on such a display.

But their exit was blocked, and there was nothing left, it seemed, but to stand and fight. So she turned and fired off a couple more arrows to good effect.

Until at last, a voice boomed out.

"Cease this! We are mourning the Pharaoh," came the voice, and she saw it came from someone dressed in flowing robes. A beautiful priestess, by the looks of it, who stared up at the two of them with wide eyes, shock filling her.

Leah held her arrow, her gaze wide at the priestess.

"We're the peaceful sort, but not when we're being cornered," she explained, lowering her bow slightly. "But we don't want to offend you when you're mourning, and mean no harm."

But it was pretty damned confusing why she could understand the woman, given the entire situation.

It's not like she spoke ancient Egyptian.

But the priestess stared up at the two of them as the guards seemed to shift uncertainly, not sure whether they should attack and overwhelm the two, or not. But when the priestess gasped and fell to her knees, bowing before the two of them, confusion ran rampant over the whole chamber.

"The Pharaoh is reborn!" she cried out, and Leah watched as the guards were further split. Some lowered their weapons, some fell to their knees too, and others kept up their vigilant guard.

Nobody could make up their mind, least of all the confused father and daughter pair.

Ten

The battle in the throne room had ended with a strange stalemate. Most of the guards eventually came around and backed down, the few that stubbornly persisted eventually left the halls entirely. And the priestess eventually guided the two of them away.

She managed to talk Leah and Monty into going through the door behind the throne--which she unlocked for them--and guided them to some rather posh chambers in the rear of the palace.

"You'll have to wait here, until I can convince the other priests to gather and confirm that you truly are the reawakened Pharaoh. Please, relax and take it easy," she said, keeping her eyes downcast, and only risking occasional glances at her father's body. "There is food and wine plenty, and more if you wish it! Just summon the servants," she said, backing out of the room without any more explanation as Leah attempted to ask her more questions to which she didn't have the answer.

And then they were alone.

"Okay, so firstly, what the absolute fuck is going on?" Leah asked as she stared at her father, her brows furrowed. Somehow the day had gone from amazing to terrifying to just very confusing, and she knew Monty wasn't likely to have any more answers than she did. She began to wander about the room, looking at the over-the-top luxury that was spread out before her. The room itself was massive, yet somehow felt cozy with all the rugs and curtains and pillows adorning it, beautiful purple, reds and blues filling the room and giving such brightness to it.

Her father didn't waste any time though, he took a rather elaborate gold chair and shoved it in front of the door. Then made an effective barricade there. Next he went around, looking to the windows, but they all peered out over the town far below, and were nothing they could escape through.

"We'll need some long, long rope to climb down from these," he said with frustration as he put his spear aside, contented at last that they weren't about to be attacked without warning, at least.

He began to study the cloth in the room, but none of it was the kind of quality of fabric you'd want to trust your life to. It was all decorative, gauzy and mostly see-through. Her father gave a few pieces a tug to test its strength, and it all tore almost instantaneously.

"Oh, you're not even the slightest bit curious whether you're really the reincarnated Pharaoh or not?" Leah asked, less desperate to escape than he was. Instead, she was inspecting the food and wine, trying to pinpoint its age. It was like trying to do an archeological dig, but with a lot less digging, and a lot better condition of the artifacts

"What?" her father said, looking to her then the food, and he joined her at the great table adorned with fresh fruit and berries. Along with several bottles of wine, some closed, one opened.

He looked stunning there, the late afternoon light pouring in through the windows, his body glistening with a sheen of perspiration from their fight. And nothing left to the imagination as he stood fully nude, his cock partially hard from the excitement. She was getting to know him enough to be intimately aware that action--violence, derring-do and more--worked her father up into a frenzy.

"We need to get out of here, before they change their mind. Or in case this is a trap," he said, lifting a fig up, smelling it, testing it for some sign of poisoning. He then saw a basin of ritual water by a window, and dumped the fruit in it, then began to wash it.

"This would be an exceptionally confusing trap. What's their end goal? Kill us? They had opportunities for that on the journey here," she said. She didn't trust the food either, but she was starving after the long walk, and she grabbed up some bread, sniffing it and taking a bite. It was delicious and sweet, and it was good to feel something in her stomach again.

"Anyways, I thought you were the adventurous type. Don't you want to find out what's going on here? This place shouldn't even *exist* anymore!"

Her father finished with the bowl of fruit, then took it back to the table before seeing she was eating the bread.

"Hey!" he said, about to snatch it from her before he sized her nude body up. He was checking for signs of poisoning, but his dick twitched all the same from the view of her large breasts, flat tummy, and ample hips. "We've gotta be careful," he said, snatching the bread away then offering her the washed figs.

"And of course I'm curious," he said. "I can only imagine... they're some holdouts of the old Egyptian ways. Maybe they ran off into the deep desert to escape modern religious customs, and keep the old ways alive," he remarked, as he began to eat some of the figs and dates.

She smirked at him, noting how his interest piqued at her nude form.

"I'm absolutely positive that they did not set this elaborate room up just to poison us in case we were able to overpower the guards," she said. "They were just as confused as us at the signs of mourning in the town, and right now, I think escape is the more dangerous option." She plucked up a fig, pushing it between her lips and letting out a moan.

"Fuck, it's so sweet..."

She had her dad wrapped around her little finger. The sound of that moan, the way she ate that fig, made his dick stiffen up to full mast as he licked his lips. He swallowed anxiously, trying to push his lust down. He ran a hand back over his hair as he continued to eat.

"Fuck I can't think," he said, as his cock bobbed. "This is like nothing I've ever been caught up in before."

"We have two choices. We can try to make it out the window, sneak through the town, kill a shit tonne of people on our way out, head into the desert, and try to find where the hell we are in the literal middle of nowhere with no compass, no supplies, and no support," she said, a smirk growing on her lips as she made him wait for the second option.

He was generally so confident, so dashing. But for a moment there, his broad shoulders hung a little low as he lifted a brow and looked to her curiously.

"The second choice...?" he asked her, his handsome face adorned with confusion instead of his usual braggadocio, that cocky half-smirk of his absent.

"The second choice is we eat, get our strength back, fuck to clear your head, and when they come back, we cautiously listen to what they have to say about you being the reincarnated Pharaoh," she grinned as she took a step towards him, her fingers tracing his jaw. "Or we could fuck first if you don't want to do it on a full stomach. I'm sure it'll take a little time for her to rally the priests together."

He took a deep breath, his chest swelling as he licked his lips and thought about what she said. But his dick was throbbing, and as close as she was, it brushed against her stomach, smearing a bit of pre-cum onto her tummy in the process.

He scratched his fingers through his hair, then popped the last of the dates in his hand into his mouth, chewing and swallowing it.

"I've eaten enough for now," he said, lowering his hand down to cup her pussy, to trail a finger along her slit. "And I need a clear head to handle the rest of this," he said as he licked his lips and cupped her breast in his other hand, fondling it.

Her grin grew wider as he so brazenly grabbed her, spoke about her as if she was just a means to an end.

"Mm, you're getting better at thinking of your little girl as your own personal cum dump," she said with such praise, even as the filthy words rolled off her tongue.

"Wanna do it at the window and let them spy on us? A bunch of them already got a front row seat, after all," she suggested.

She saw her father's head furrow as he thought about her filthy, depraved suggestion. He looked poised to reject it out of hand, and said, "That's insane. We'd be inviting more trouble and--" but his finger curled up, parting her folds, finding a reservoir of her slick honey inside her pussy as his dick throbbed and he shivered with desire.

"Y-yeah," he said after a moment's delay, swallowing anxiously. "C'mon, I need to clear my head so I can get us out of this," he said as he led her towards the window.

It was a bit harder for her to walk, given how he was holding her, but somehow they managed, and soon, he had her leaned up against the edge of the window. Beneath them, the town sprawled outwards far into the distance, the white limestone shimmering against the golden sand as the sun began to dip lower along the horizon. It bathed them in its beautiful light, letting their toned bodies glimmer with the slickness of their fear and arousal.

He placed a hand between her shoulder blades, and guided her to bend over the window sill. It protruded out of the room slightly, into what might be considered a mini-balcony, which gave the town below a better view of them as he grasped his cock in his free hand, raising it up to glide along her puffy slit.

"Fuck, I need to cum bad," he grunted, as he unceremoniously pushed the head of his cock inside her.

She moaned, nothing about his more utilitarian words doing anything to dissuade her own pleasure.

"Oh, you don't just need to cum," she said, pushing her

ass against him as she looked out over the town. "You need to breed your little girl. You already know your hand won't do any longer," she taunted him, her legs spreading as she pushed herself up higher.

His two hands went to her hips, and he grasped her ass cheeks in the process, peeling them back so that with one hard thrust he hilted himself up into her completely. He moaned, that thick hard cock shoved in deep as he began to help himself to her body, pumping into her with his needy thrusts as he sighed contentedly, as if just being inside her had released such a desperate need already.

"Y-yeah," he confessed as his hips smacked against her ass cheeks. "This is what I need... my little girl on my dick," he said with a moan. "Fuck... nothing compares to your pussy, sweetie," he said, his voice rumbly and low.

Her smile grew wider as he confessed his filthiest desires, praised her to high heavens. Her expression was almost angelic as she looked out the window, feeling him hilting inside her so quickly. She had worn down his defenses so quickly, and she was luxuriating in the knowledge of how much power and control she had over him.

And how easily she was able to get what she needed from him.

But an added little twist was the fact she could see people below in the streets, and guards stationed about, beginning to notice them. Her father's eyes were shut as he pumped into her pussy, his groin slapping against her ass and making those thick, supple cheeks ripple and quake as he grunted and moaned.

She got the full view of those starry eyed denizens of

this new Ancient Egypt staring up at her, as her own father claimed her carnally.

"You belong to daddy... don't you?" he grunted out, licking his lips as he moaned and his dick twitched, spurting pre-cum into her.

It was such a high, and she forced herself not to look away, not to even close her eyes as he took her from behind. Instead, she just started moaning more loudly, performing a little bit for all the voyeurs below.

"As long as you behave," she teased, licking her lips as she pushed her ass into his hips.

He moaned, his muscular form tensing up as he hammered into her harder, rocking her body, making her heavy tits jiggle and sway over the edge of the railing. He gasped and shivered as his balls swung up to slap loudly against her mound.

"Ah... ah, I'll... I'll do whatever it takes to keep you mine," he said, his bare feet planted wide as he fucked her with such a raw, fast pace. "I'll keep you... swollen and pregnant for the rest of my days, just so you have to stay mine," he grunted, his adonis-like body glistening in the open daylight as the crowd below grew.

And as it did, her moans turned to groans, then to screams, her expression contorted in an exaggerated way, like a stage actress performing for the crowd.

But the emotions behind it were all sincere, and she couldn't fake the orgasm that was fast building in her clit. It throbbed painfully, her own arousal and need enough to rival his. She definitely took after him when it came to the fact that fear and arousal were close friends for her, and always made her body more sensitive and receptive to stimulus.

The fact her father's heavy, cum-laden balls kept smacking against her sensitive clit was only fueling that dizzying high. And he kept up his assault on her pussy, fast and hard, and only coming on more intensely with each passing moment.

"Al--... almost there," he gasped out, as he gripped her smooth, flawless flesh tighter, his thrusting becoming more intense as he opened his eyes to gaze down and see the great audience they'd amassed. It shocked him, and made his whole body tremble with excitement that everyone got to see him fucking his daughter.

He'd engaged in public antics, in pleasure dens and such, but nothing approaching this level of debauchery. And it thrilled him, made him moan loudly.

"Everyone knows what a pervert you are, dad, and they like it. I like it," she moaned, holding onto the railing and arching her back for him. It let her heavy tits bounce forward, the additional sensation only teasing her higher towards ecstasy.

"We were interrupted earlier. Fill me with your cum and I won't lose a drop this time," she cried out.

He gasped and panted, moaning aloud as he fucked her with renewed vigor. He was insatiable for her, and her taunting, her teasing only made him worse.

"Gonna c-cum," he gasped out, then without pausing, or even slowing his thrusting, he started to shoot off his load. Thick ropes of pearly white seed flooding her depths as he howled out loudly into the late afternoon sky, blasting his load deep into his young daughter, flooding her fertile depths for all to witness as he shuddered and quaked.

His pleasure traveled through to her, and sent her over the edge. She screamed, not holding anything back as her body yielded to his. She loved this, loved him, loved everyone knowing what hedonistic perverts they were, and the orgasm that spread through her that time was something special.

Perhaps it was the luxurious surroundings, or the fact that once more they were facing life or death peril, or just that they had amassed such an audience... It just made her feel like a Queen, someone of great importance. And that was an aphrodisiac in and of itself.

It helped draw out the pleasure of the moment, as her father thrust into her without pause, and continued to shoot every last drop of his seed into her. If her father was Pharaoh, then she was at least a Queen, right? And bent over, receiving his seed for all to see, she felt like one. Truly.

Her father grunted, shuddered, and moaned as his thrusts finally began to slow, his climax almost over. And then... behind them, they heard the sound of a gasp, from a voice that was all too close.

Eleven

T here he was, balls deep inside his own daughter, his dick still twitching as it spurt the last of its seed into her... as not only the entire town below watched, but an assembly of priests stood in shocked silence behind them.

"It's true..." gasped one of the priests.

"How did you get in here?!" Monty demanded in shock, still gripping Leah's hips.

Leah, meanwhile, leaned forward on the railing, giggling as she tried to catch her breath.

"If you wanted a front row seat, it's still polite to say something. But I guess your people are really stealthy, huh? Second time this happened today."

Monty didn't find it quite so funny as her, judging by the furrow in his brow as he looked between Leah and the watching priests. But he also didn't yank his cock out either, as it twitched thickly and let off one final big dollop of cum inside her pussy.

"It's not what it looks like--" Monty began.

"His own daughter..." muttered one of the priests, as they began to shuffle back out of the room, hushed mutterings passing between them as they exited out of a door that had been hidden behind a tapestry that Monty had missed in his search of the chambers.

Leah bit down on her lower lip, trying to hold back her amused laughter. She had none of his shame, and mostly found his own embarrassment to be delicious.

"Uh-oh, dad, you're in trouble," she teased.

The familiar priestess who had first brought an end to the violence in the throne room went wide eyed at Leah's words, but then exited the room after the other priests.

And a moment too late, Monty finally pulled his dick out of his daughter's pussy and rushed towards that door as it slammed shut.

"Dammit!" he said, as he pounded his fist on the stonework there. "Did you really need to make it worse?" he asked her.

Leah made a disgruntled sound as he pulled from her, her brows furrowing in annoyance.

"Do you really think they were going to kill us before but you'd say it's not what they think and they'd apologize and send us on our way?" She followed after him, once more drooling her seed down her toned thighs. "I let you have your kink, why can't you at least let me appreciate mine before they off-with-their-heads us?"

Monty looked practically irate.

"Off with our heads? I'm not letting them do that! You're my daughter! What kind of father would I be if I let you die here? And you're probably carrying my child by now!" he said, as he searched the stone door for some crack, or exploit he could use to get it open.

Leah let out a sigh, watching him try to find an escape.

"Well, at least your brain is working again. We should have tried to make time for a quickie on the walk over here and we would have caught that other door right away," she said, unable to suppress her amusement at it all. "Come on, we escaped an awful hell beast worm in the desert, we'll escape this too."

She saw out of the corner of her eyes, some clothes the locals wore, though far more embellished and elaborate. It was probably garments for the old Pharaoh and his wife or... whatever, she was no archaeologist.

"You're right," he said, as he crouched down in the nude, still feeling along the door for something to exploit, the tiniest of cracks. "We're getting out of here," he said with a smile, a glint in his eyes as he looked up to her. "Because we're an unstoppable duo, we Barnes."

She smiled.

"There's the man I fell in love with," she said, wandering over to the clothes to pick it up and see if it would fit. The fabric was delicate, but well made, and she held the feminine dress up against her body. The torso was wide, clearly not intended to cover the breasts, and dipped low down to her bellybutton before draping off into an asymmetric train along her left leg.

"Might feel better in some clothes. What do you think, is it my style?"

He was busy fumbling with something at the bottom of the door as he grunted and said, "Yeah, that's a good idea. It'll help us not get identified the moment we're spotted on the streets." But as his gaze drifted over towards her, seeing her hold that scandalous garment up--which itself was practically see-through--he froze.

And she saw his dick twitch again at the sight of her.

"Real... real good idea," he said, licking his lips and swallowing.

Her lips twitched in amusement.

"Yea, I thought you'd like that. And luckily, I think what they have for you is just as nice," she said, setting the dress aside and grabbing what she imagined was meant for the Pharaoh. It was made of slightly thicker material, not as transparent, but it had a gorgeous sheen to the purple fabric. It was open on one side, and she imagined it was to tie at the hip, leaving part of his leg and ass somewhat exposed.

He stood up and walked towards her, looking at the garment curiously.

"Well, better than nothing, huh?" he said as he held it up and then started to pull it on. The fabric was inlaid with gold thread, and small emeralds and rubies sewn into patterns. And when he put it on, it left little to the imagination. His bare chest mostly exposed, and his half his hard ass left hanging out.

Hell, with as big a package as her father had, that too was left partially exposed whenever he moved in certain ways. Like when he slipped on the royal, gem-studded sandals.

"I've got good news," he said.

"I agree," she said, watching him dress before she seemed to realize he wasn't talking about what she thought he was talking about. Her gaze went up to his. "Wait, what?"

He gave her a bemused smile as he saw her gaze, and where it was lingering.

"You should get dressed. Now," he said to her, tossing her the last of her things, before he picked up the head dress that went with his clothes. It was purple as well, with a gold snake adornment at the head of it. "This'll make it a lot more difficult to tell I'm not one of the locals," he said.

She let out another giggle, even as she started to wrap the gossamer gown around herself. Just as she expected, it left her tits exposed, the edges seeming to push the heavy mounds together and giving her some extra cleavage.

"Hey how weird is it that this is the first time we're seeing each other in clothes since I told you who I was?" she asked as she began putting some bracelets on her wrists.

"If you can call this clothes," he said as he stared blatantly at her perfectly presented tits. That thick shaft of his twitching beneath his gauzy fabric. But then he made his way back to the door, and bent down, his hand moving around the bottom. "But all the same, you look good dressed up," he remarked with a grin.

"You just better not tear this off of me. It's so pretty," she said as she found that there were anklets and sandals to go with the outfit as well, and they seemed to almost be fitted for her body exactly. It was a little unnerving, but also... it felt nice to get all dressed up after countless days in the middle of nowhere.

"I wonder if they have that black eyeliner that all the Egyptians had in art..." she said, starting to search around for a vanity.

She found it, in spades. Such an elaborate vanity decked out with all manner of powders and lip stains, a trove of it.

And as she found that, her father got up and looked around the room, until he found a metal rod, adorned with gold and silver, and a cobra at the top. He took it back to the door, working on prying it open.

"I think I can get this open..." he said.

Leah opened one of the pots of color, dabbing the red stain on her lips and smiling at her reflection. She then found a brush and some kohl, wetting the tip and beginning to trace along the edges of her eyes.

"Let me know if you need help."

But her father was stubborn, as she predicted. And as he grunted and groaned, she had ample time to finish with her makeup. Until at last... she heard the stone slide, and the door open. She turned back to see her father standing there with a triumphant grin on his face, that golden rod in his hand.

"Told you I'd get us out of here," he said with a cocky look. And even with his eyes stopping at her tits again for a while, he managed to note her new makeup. "Good look," he said.

She smiled at him brightly, grabbing a few more of the washed dates and a bit of the bread and butter.

"We should find a little bag, take some cheese and wine with us for the journey," she said, beginning to look for something she could easily fashion into a sack.

He looked around, then went to one of the windows. He pulled down one of the gauzy curtains, and then went to her in turn. He tied it around her arm and shoulder, fashioning a crude carrying bag, then he touched his hand to her cheek and spoke to her sweetly.

"We're going to get out of this. And I'm going to do everything in my power to protect you, and keep you safe. So you have a long, happy, healthy life, with many of your own kids," he said, his voice so rich with conviction and determination, with love and commitment.

It would've been such a sweet, powerful moment, but his other hand had managed to find its way up to cup her breast and caress it. Though judging by the look on his face he hadn't realized he'd started doing it.

She leaned in, kissing his mouth, smiling all the while.

"I'm glad you've decided to go all the way in. I was worried there for a while," she said, touching the back of his hand that was playing with her tit. "It's so much more fun this way."

Only then did he seem to realize what he was doing, as his eyes went to her hand, atop his, and he stiffened. In more ways than one. And his eyes went wide. But he didn't yank it away, he stared at it a moment, then wet his lips.

"What can I say?" he said with a shrug of his broad shoulders. "I'm addicted to your pussy... and your tits, it seems," he remarked with another longing gaze at her ample breast, resting heavily against his palm.

She leaned in to him again, kissing his mouth, tracing her tongue along the seam of his lips.

"I'm addicted to you too. Maybe we can go find an inn in town, hide there for a few days..." she smiled, her nose brushing against his. "A little safe place to really indulge."

He kissed her back, warm and passionately, the two of them enjoying that final moment before they made their escape. His hand squeezed her breast tighter, making the flesh swell between his digits, and his thumb teased her areola, getting it oh so stiff.

"Thank you for curing me of my delusions," he said, their lips smacking together, his voice low and husky. "Because I really want to see your pregnant belly and tits plastered in my cum," he remarked as if it was such a sweet, romantic thing to say.

"Me too," she murmured back, her fingers running through his thick hair, tucking it behind his ear under the elaborate headdress. "Let's grab our things and make our way out of here, because if we stay like this any longer, you're gonna be fucking me again, and they're going to be sneaking in to watch us, again. I can't handle the humiliation of having someone best us thrice in one day."

He smiled then seemed to snap back into reality, "Right," he said, swallowing and adjusting his robes in a futile effort to hide the thick erection he was sporting. But he went about their business, gathering some of the dates and figs and other snacks, putting them into her makeshift bag, then making his own.

And before long they were ready, and he nodded to her most seriously, as she gripped her bow and arrows again.

They snuck out through the door, maintaining quiet footsteps as they entered the dark hallway. And up ahead some rays of orange light came in, from the setting sun. The hall was overshadowed by giant statues of huge men and women, with animal heads or else elaborate head-dresses.

They pushed on by it, her father taking the lead, his spear and scepter in hand as they made their way down, down towards the lit exit at the far end.

"Be ready," he murmured to her quietly, his ass half hanging out of that garb as he moved in front of her.

"Mhm," she murmured back, her body alert as she tried to make sense of the layout of the building, listening for how sound travelled.

They came to the door, but after so long in that dark hallway, they couldn't make out much of what was on the other side. But they could hear a voice, booming and loud.

"If this was truly the reincarnation of the Pharaoh, he would be here now to tell us as much! He is a cheap, foreign imposter," declared the voice, as the sound of many voices engaged in hushed muttering.

"We all saw their display! It was nothing less than the audacity of the Pharaoh himself. And we know his royal proclivities as the Sun God," said a female voice, to more murmuring of a crowd unseen.

Leah stilled, listening with such an intense, scrutinizing stare towards the source of the arguments. Royal proclivities as the Sun God? What was that supposed to mean? Though she was right, her father *did* have royal audacity.

They edged closer, to try and get an actual look at the other side, but a rich tapestry blocked much of their view. Or perhaps it was just a curtain, it was hard to tell from their perspective.

"They sullied the Pharaoh's royal preserve! Where only he may hunt and gather and lounge," said the male voice again.

"Further proof that it is truly the Pharaoh! He reincarnated in the very place he loved most, with his beloved sister at his side," said the woman's voice.

"It's his daughter! Not his sister!" said the other voice.

"It is close enough, just a side effect of the holy resurrection," said the woman, as her father slipped on his royal sandals a little and teetered.

As Leah moved to try and right him, she stepped on her own flowing skirts, and tripped. And together the two of them stumbled forward, tangled up in each other, through the curtains to stand before the enormous crowd on the other side. And the court of judges deliberating their fate.

Twelve

There they stood, father and daughter, adorned in holy garb as the crowd gasped. Priests stood around them, debating their case originally, but then shocked into silence as the pair stood boldly before them and all the people of that isolated civilization.

They'd never seen so many wide eyes and slack jawed stares in their days. At least, not all at once.

"The Pharaoh is here to tell you of his reincarnation, having escaped from the room that was made specifically to his needs, and yet you stand here, filled with *doubt?!*" Leah cried out, trying to regain her composure and put her high school drama classes to good use.

Monty looked to her, surprised by Leah's sudden grasp of the situation. But he puffed up his chest, looked out at the crowd and tried to pump himself up for the task.

He looked out at the sea of expectant and shocked faces, then raised a hand to the sound of countless gasps. He realized it was probably the scepter he held in his hand a moment after that.

"The Sun God Ra has returned!" He declared, that being the best he could come up with in the moment. And at that moment, the setting sun hit the exact point where it shone in through the windows, and reflected off the mirrored metal surfaces, to coalesce onto him, setting him in gleaming sunlight.

And the people gasped and cried out in shock, and the priestess who had been arguing their cause all along, fell to her knees, bowing before him in a display of obedience. One of the other priests even slowly began to fall to his knees to do the same, as most of the audience followed suit.

Leah wasn't quite certain what was expected of her, as sister of the Pharaoh, but she decided that she'd remain upright, stood at Monty's side, and glaring at those who didn't seem quite ready to kneel.

"The souls of these foreigners were easy for us to oust, and it meant that none of our people had to be forced on. Our warriors did well to find them for the Pharaoh when he saw his end was drawing near!"

Monty looked to her, astonished by her nerve. And her ability to make up bullshit on the spot. He watched a priest stand up, ready to argue and insult them. But Monty pointed his scepter at the man and glared intimidatingly.

"All things make sense in the light of the Sun God," he said, seemingly willing the man to sit back down. "It is my holy duty to marry my sister, and continue the long tradition of Pharaohs past," he said, "but when I had to rebirth myself into a new form... I needed my dear sister-wife with me. And I arranged to birth her new form myself. As her brother, father and husband, all together. Such is the will of

126

Ra!" he declared, as even more stragglers gasped and fell to their knees before them.

At that point, only one priest even resisted kneeling and bowing low.

Leah looked at him like he was lower than dirt, her dark eyeliner making her narrow gaze even more menacing.

"You know the price of doubt in the Hall of Osiris," Leah said, recalling what little she did know about the Egyptians. It wasn't a major interest to her, but she did find the different beliefs of the afterlife to be somewhat of a fascination. She vaguely remembered a sort of journey that one had to take after death, and it ended in the place of judgment, in the Hall of Osiris. Her memory got a little spotty after that.

The crowd gasped, and it seemed as if every last one of them had cast their eyes down in reverence. And finally, that last, hold out priest trembled, averted his eyes, and fell to the floor.

And with everyone's gaze turned away from them, her father looked to her with a surprised expression.

"It's working," he muttered to her quietly, before clearing his throat and noting that the sun had almost set entirely, and he'd soon be without any glow on him at all. "Go, my subjects. Return to your business. For I have returned to set things right. To return justice to its proper form. I shall mend all errors and mistakes, make right all wrongs! So sayeth the Sun God," he remarked, before turning and grasping Leah's arm to lead her back into the tunnel.

She was only too grateful to be getting out of there, and

scurried at his side, her heart thudding so loud in her chest she was afraid that the entire room would hear it.

But once they were beyond the curtain, and into that private hall, they were free to speak again.

"Holy shit," her father said to her, still holding her arm as they walked. "I can't believe you pulled that off," he said with a proud grin on his face.

"I can't either. Fuck, we're gonna need some excuses. Foreigners' brains are too small, they couldn't hold all our memories? Wait, did the Egyptians believe brains were where thoughts were held or the hearts? It's been too long..." she muttered to him, her footsteps quick, eager to head back to the relative privacy of the room they'd so eagerly fled.

"I'm just glad I remembered that the Pharaoh's practiced incest. Every ruler paired with their sibling," he said to her, "then I just had to think up an excuse for why you were calling me 'daddy' instead of 'big brother'," he remarked with a grin as they reached their posh chamber again, though it seemed a little less like a prison, this time.

"Big brother doesn't really roll off the tongue, but yea, your story was good. I'm glad you were able to roll with it, because that was pretty terrifying. You must be stiff as a board under there."

He laughed and cracked a wry grin at her, before glancing down at the tent in his loose flowing robes.

"No kidding," he said with a lick of his lips as he put the scepter down on the table at the center of the room. "But I like 'daddy' better anyhow," he said, with a glint in his eye as he sized her up again with obvious interest. The hand that reached out to cup and caress her breast was a dead giveaway.

"No more thoughts of escaping for now, then?" she asked, her eyes twinkling as she looked up at him with such affection and lust. "Just going to defile some more of this room and enjoy ourselves for a lavish night of debauchery?"

Her father grinned and squeezed her breast, but as his mouth opened to speak... she heard only a woman's voice.

"Please forgive me great Pharaoh," came the priestesses voice, as she fell down, bowing low before them both. "I am ever your humble servant," said the woman who had been arguing on their behalf, and saved them from the guards hours before.

Leah's brows shot up, her lips parting in surprise. How was she so damned stealthy?

"Your service will be remembered," Leah finally managed, but with her father's hand on her tit, she was not quite in the mood for small talk about Pharaoh stuff.

"Thank you, Great Royal Wife," said the priestess, still down low on the floor and refusing to look up. "I ask for nothing, though. I only wish to serve you both to the best of my abilities, such is my fate," she said.

While Monty arched a brow and looked rather perplexed.

"You seem a great candidate to become the new High Priest," Monty said, smiling politely, even as his hand fondled Leah's supple breast. "The faith needs ones such as you, who are committed to what is right and true, above their own station," he remarked.

Leah looked at Monty, at how willing he was to touch

her, even in front of another, and her heart began to thud louder in her chest. He was so quickly embracing their twisted romance, and the excitement that it filled her with was almost too much to bear.

"I am unworthy of such a great responsibility, oh Pharaoh," she said on the floor as Monty continued fondling Leah's breast.

"Not if we say so," he remarked with a cocky grin again. "Now, uh... we could use some privacy here, I think?" he remarked, looking to Leah with an arched brow.

Leah smiled at him, leaning in and giving him a kiss on his mouth before kissing up towards his ear.

"Perhaps she can help fill in some of those gaps in our memories," she whispered before pulling back, looking at him curiously.

Monty's brows rose, and he looked to Leah with a blossoming grin as he marveled at her craftiness.

"But first," he said, as the priestess had begun to slunk away. "Rise up," he said, bidding her to do so as she stood up almost immediately. "Answer some of our questions. For the process of reincarnation has left our memories a little foggy, in certain areas," he said, still holding Leah close.

"Of course, Great Pharaoh," she said, hands over her heart, head bowed. "But... would you rather not do so in your private chambers than your waiting room for the grand temple?" she said.

"Certainly. We just returned to grab a few things we'd forgotten in our haste to meet with the priests, and then got distracted in trying out our new bodies," Leah said, quickly thinking on her feet. She then grabbed for a bracelet she'd not taken the first time around.

And Monty picked up his scepter again.

"Lead the way," he said to the priestess when she delayed a moment, waiting for them to do so.

Off she went, guiding them through the halls of the giant, limestone palace again. Down corridors, around corners, passing numerous guards who all fell to one knee at their passing, giving a salute as they kept their eyes downcast.

"I will have your servants sent in right away, to attend to all of your needs, Great Pharaoh," the priestess said, after the dizzying guide through the palace came to an end, and they arrived at the most absurdly decadent room they'd ever seen.

Great columns all around, with silks and cushions strewn across the room strategically, to heighten its beauty. Great riches, art and a feast of food that made the other room appear destitute by comparison.

A great throne sat at the head, but it was more like a bed really, with a giant golden backboard.

"Damn..." said Monty, sizing up the stunning display.

"It's good to be back where you belong," Leah said with a smile, flitting about the room as she inspected it. "We must have made the journey through the other side quickly, so little has changed," she hazarded a guess, given that the town was still in mourning when they arrived.

Monty drifted through the room slower, marveling at it with the eyes of an archaeologist.

"Indeed, Great Royal Wife," said the priestess as she stood there near the center of the room, looking so humble and obedient. "You left the mortal coil but a night ago. So quick was your ascent from the Underworld, praise Anubis," she said.

"Of course we weren't long," said Monty. "I would not want my people to suffer from uncertainty... or worse," he remarked.

"Yes. Some of the priests said your lack of an heir was a grievous oversight, or... or worse," the priestess remarked, clearly embarrassed by the talk. "But they will surely see now, that you were saving your powers to reincarnate you and your Great Royal Wife whole. To spare us the transition."

"Let it never be said that he didn't have a plan. But I'm sure much has happened in the past night with our trades and all that. A formal report of the recent happenings of the past month shall be readied for the Pharaoh for tomorrow morning, of course?" Leah said as she stopped at one of the dressers, opening it and looking inside at the array of lingerie inside.

"Of course, Great Royal Wife," said the priestess with a curtsey. "I will have the serving girls sent in with your favorites, as well. And to prepare your makeup and dress for you," she said obediently. "Is there anything else I can do to help you both, my Pharaoh's?" she asked, batting her long lashes as she stood there, looking elegant and petite compared to Leah.

"Make sure everything's tested before it's given to us. I don't want it to be poisoned," Monty said with a smile as he walked up to that giant throne, then sat himself down on it, knees spread and mistakenly splaying his cock and balls to the priestess who blushed.

Leah just found it amusing how easily he seemed to forget himself, or perhaps just roll with the new persona he was taking on. Either way, she enjoyed the view.

"Yes, the moments before death are hazy, so any information you have on the illness will help the Pharaoh piece together what happened."

"Of course, Great Royal wife. And I shall be sure to prepare your usual for the morning," the Priestess said as she turned to leave, though Leah was sure she caught something in the young woman's eye, as she peered longingly at her father, Monty.

Suddenly things weren't so amusing, and a pang of jealousy struck through her. She was able to hold it back, though, as the Priestess headed towards the door. At least in as much as she didn't immediately fly into a blind rage and threaten the tenuous peace they'd secured. But she went to her father's side, possessive of him as she blocked the view of him from the Priestess' path.

The priestess paused momentarily in the doorway, to peer back longingly at the 'Pharaoh' but by then Leah was in the way.

Monty, for his part, seemed oblivious and he just smiled up at Leah warmly, reaching out to take her hand and tug her closer to him.

"Not a bad spot to hold up for a while, huh?" he said with some wry amusement as he gazed up at her.

"We could have done worse," she agreed, her arms wrapping around him affectionately, possessively. "We're still on dangerous ground, but nothing we can't navigate together, right?"

As she leaned one knee onto the throne-bed, and put her arms around him, he wrapped his around her waist, holding her close as he smiled to her. Then he just sort of casually nuzzled her breasts, then kissed one.

"It's a lot better than hiding out in an inn and slumming it undercover, at least," he said, before wrapping his lips around one nipple and beginning to suckle softly at it, his eyes shutting as he enjoyed her body.

Leah finally heard the Priestess leave, the door closing behind her, and her shoulders relaxed somewhat.

"It is much better," she purred, her hand stroking along the back of his head, down his neck, encouraging him to taste her tit in a slow, leisurely manner. "Though the Priestess does seem to have a special interest in you."

Monty was wrapped up in enjoying her breast, so he was slow to realize what she said. His eyes fluttered open, and he peered up at Leah, before pulling off her breast, letting her nipple snap into place atop that large mound of supple, smooth flesh.

"She does?" he asked, surprised as his hand slid down over her ass, caressing it, squeezing it.

"She does," Leah confirmed, frowning slightly. "Did I say to stop sucking me?" she asked as she lifted her heavy breast back up towards him, still glistening with saliva around the stiff nipple. "I imagine it won't be long before she tries to get you somewhere private."

"Unfortunately for her, I'm married," he said with a cheeky grin, before obeying and taking that offered tit. His hungry mouth more ravenously enveloping it this time, suckling and swirling his tongue around that sensitive teat, as his two strong hands fondle and grope at her thick, round ass. A soft hum of a moan escaping his lips and vibrating through her breast.

She relaxed into his body, letting him feel of her, taste of her, and allowing her to simply luxuriate in the more sensual pleasures of her form. It was another long day, but he always seemed to be able to give her energy.

"Yes, you are. And you found a way to make our honeymoon even more special."

As she watched her father suckle ravenously at her tit, from out of two side entrances, a stream of servants came pouring out. They held platters of food, casks of wine, and some of them just carried cloth and other things, it all happened so smoothly and silently that Monty wasn't even aware, as his eyes were shut. And the servants seemed to pay no heed to their lascivious act, as a dancer even came in and took up a spot in the center of the room.

Another servant began to pluck upon some harp like instrument, and that was when Monty's eyes opened up, aware of what was going on, just as the dancer started to move.

"It's okay, we just have some company, apparently," Leah said, still stroking his head, her body leaning in against him. Having people constantly around them was going to get old quick, but she was determined not to let it ruin the calm, sensual mood of the moment.

Another dancer came out to join the first, making it a pair: a boy and girl. They were dressed in relatively little. Unless you counted the gold chains and piercings. The rest was three triangles of fabric over the woman's breasts and vagina, and a loose dangling strip of cloth on the male, and a tight little garment that wouldn't even qualify as briefs underwear back home, just a tight cupping of his package.

One of the servants came and opened a sealed bottle of wine beside the throne, then poured up a glass. A tester tried some, then a glass was offered up to Leah.

She smiled at the tester, accepting the glass.

"Thank you," she said on instinct, before wondering if the Great Royal Wife would even know of such words. But she figured politeness was never a bad thing, and simply went back to stroking Monty's head as she glanced over the room. How could someone ever get used to this level of servitude?

Another servant came and began to offer her delicious fruits, as Monty suckled and fondled her body. Until she was caught off guard, finding one of the servants coming up behind her, touching her! Until she realized the serving girl was helping adjust her dress skirts so they weren't blocking access to her slit.

And another reached down to tug her father's loin cloth aside, revealing his thick, hard shaft. The sight of which earned a gasp of surprise from the servant.

It was definitely... weird. Not in a bad way, Leah supposed, but it was very strange to have such minor details handled for her. It was more challenging to try to blend in as the Pharaoh and his Great Royal Wife then, compared to in the Priest's hall. It was all just so much more intimate and confusing.

And suddenly, as she pondered it all, and let her eyes move around the room, soaking in the ambiance, the dancers, she heard the sound of a dick being pumped. Right before her.

And Leah looked down to see one of the serving girl's dainty hands on her father's thick cock. That hand pumping his shaft as he moaned, eyes shut, producing a bead of glistening, clear pre-cum at the tip as he moaned and shuddered.

"Hey, that's my job!" Leah said with more petulance than she intended. Do all royals let the servants take all the fun out of life for them?

Her father's eyes opened then he peered down, and pulled off Leah's tit in shock as he saw it wasn't her hand on his dick. But the serving girl stared up at them both with wide-eyed shock. As if she'd done nothing wrong or out of place.

"I... so s-sorry, Pharaoh and Great Royal Wife," she said, down-casting her eyes. "I was just attempting to keep the Pharaoh ready for you, as usual," she said, worry in her voice.

"His new body seems able to get ready much easier than the last one," Leah assured her. "You're doing fine. You just don't need to worry about that any longer as part of your tasks," Leah said, her voice softening after the shock wore off.

Monty looked a little awkward, but his dick was still throbbing with desire as a servant placed a golden goblet of wine in his open hand. He arched a brow, then began to drink from it as the serving girl backed away.

"Clearly he does not need my lowly attentions," the serving girl said as she backed off. "You are like the goddess Isis herself, Great Royal Wife," she said respectfully.

That made Leah earnestly smile.

"You are too sweet," she said affectionately, before taking a small sip of her wine, enjoying the strange, exotic taste of it. "I suppose you've been serving the Pharaoh for... how long has it been?"

"Most of my life, Great Royal Wife," she said as she bowed to Leah, and Monty sat there, sipping some wine, then leaning in to lick at Leah's untouched teat, giving it a brief suckle as the girls chatted. "It has been the greatest honor of my life to assist our living gods," she said.

"You've done well to so eagerly return to your post. I know that change is a beautiful part of life, but can also lead to its own challenges," Leah said, trying to sound as refined as she could. "There will be more changes, for the Pharaoh has returned with greater insight and knowledge, and more understanding of the path for our people."

The girl's eyes sparkled, the dancers moved with such grace, and all around Leah there was such decadence and opulence.

"I have faith in you both," said the serving girl as she glanced up at Leah with a smile on her beautiful young face. "And if there is ever anything I can do for you, Great Royal Wife, you need but tell me and I will eagerly see it done. If ever the Pharaoh's great desires grow too much for you to bear, I am your servant, willing to step in and take your place in such a time of need," she said.

And Monty arched a brow at that, leaning back in his throne and drinking some more wine as he looked between Leah and the servant.

"Yeah, if I ever become too much for you," Monty said with a wry grin.

"Might be more of a challenge if I become too much for him. But I am certain that soon an heir will be on its way," Leah said, her teasing smirk trained on Monty. "And I've heard that lusts only grow at that point."

Monty's brows rose in surprise at that--surprise and titillation--as his cock throbbed thickly in the air. He licked his lips and swallowed, then followed it up with more wine, which a servant immediately refilled.

"I plan to produce a great many heirs now, actually," he said as he licked his lips and peered up at Leah's face, her breasts. Admiring her beauty all over.

"Another reason for your great plan, to form me from yourself. To make sure that I was ready for your heirs," Leah grinned, adding to his own story about why she wasn't his sister-wife. It was fun to concoct so many kinky fantasies, to tease each other with. But having it be a part of the local cannon added an additional layer of excitement.

"Indeed," Monty said as he gripped Leah's ass tighter, pulling her in closer as they both drank wine and ate the offered fruit that was dangled into their mouths for them. "I had to re-create my bride to be perfect, so she could successfully carry many, many of my children," he said with a grin. "And look at how amazingly perfect she is," he said with stars in his eyes.

And the servants all seemed to take that as a directive, and looked at Leah with such intense attention.

"Your Great Royal Wife is so perfect, Pharaoh. Beautiful and seductive, in every way," said the male dancer and his partner.

It wasn't long ago that Leah was a virgin, but that seemed a life time ago. In the lives they were living, it truly was. But in such a short amount of time, Monty had unlocked every suppressed desire, every secret lust, every deviant kink. So as an entire room, stared at her exposed form, filling her with praise, it only heightened her own arousal.

"Mm, made just for you," Leah purred, leaning in to kiss him.

Monty kissed her back, the two of them passionate and affectionate, the fact that a room full of servants were watching doing nothing to dilute their enthusiasm for each other. His dick just throbbed, and he fondled and kissed her.

"Made you perfect, just for my own personal use," he rumbled to her in between kisses, as he grabbed her two ass cheeks and pulled her over his lap.

She shifted to pin his cock between them, grinding her hips to tease his flesh against her bare mons.

"Mhm," she murmured between kisses, her tongue teasing his as her arms hugged him close. "I can't wait to swell with your child. Your heir."

His hands squeezed her two thick ass cheeks, making her supple flesh swell between his long fingers. And he moaned as they kissed and she ground against his dick, their lips smacking all the while.

"My bride, my daughter... my sister," he husked out between their kissing. "You'll swell up with many, many of my heirs," he said with a grin teasing his lips as he moaned deeply with want and desire. "I'll keep you pregnant for the rest of my days," he boasted.

"This time, maybe I'll actually be able to keep your

entire load in me, instead of having to be marched around just after you pop," she teased, her kisses moving up his jaw towards his ear, licking the cusp of it. "I hate wasting a single drop."

Those words, and how seductive they sounded, sent a shiver down his spine. He trembled with desire as his dick swelled painfully large with need. He moaned aloud, gripping her tighter in his hands.

"Maybe I'll have the servants tie you down, so you can't even accidentally spill a drop," he said, his voice heavier, rumbly with lust and want. "Have you spend the rest of your days tied down and pregnant," he said, giving her ass cheek a slap for all the servants to see.

"Maybe for a night or two," she teased, giggling a little. "But you'll never have to tie me down. You know I'll be a good girl, as long as you're good to me."

He moaned and kissed her deeply, ravenous at the idea of his good little girl, so devoted and into him. He opened his eyes to glance around, see that all the servants had stopped and were watching them, as if part of their regular duties were to give the royal couple their full attention when they were rutting.

"You're the perfect girl for me," Monty said, breathing heavier, as he gripped her ass and hips, trying to guide her to get onto his dick. "I made you with my own dick to be that way, didn't I?" he said, enjoying getting into their roles.

"We fit together too perfectly for it to be any other way," she said, pulling back enough to look into his eyes. She stared at him as her hips lifted, letting him position his crown to her wet lips. "Of course you made me, daddy."

Their eyes locked so intensely in that moment, some deep inner truth passed between them. Their love and desire for each other deeper than anything they'd put into words before, and even as they gazed so longingly at each other, he guided her down, so that her puffy, glistening labia flowered around his shaft and he groaned lowly as he stretched her pussy out wide.

"I made you... for me," he said, his voice a bit strained as he shuddered and licked his lips. "My sweet little girl... I could never go back to life without you," he confessed.

"You'll never have to," she moaned, her pussy descending along his shaft, the two of them working in tandem to fit their toned bodies together. It was so strange to have such an intimate, personal moment be observed by so many. It wasn't like before, where Leah was goading him to exhibitionism. It was so much deeper than that.

"I love you," she whispered in his ear, kissing him there. "I'll never let you get away from me."

He shuddered at her declaration, a deep, longing shudder. He held her by the ass, his fingers curling in under her thighs as helped her ride his dick up and down, that shaft glistening whenever it withdrew from her. He moaned and kissed her slender neck, declaring in return, "I love you, my little girl... you're mine forever. I swear it."

But the servants had grown confused by the royal couple tending to themselves so completely, and a pair of servants had appeared at Leah's side, reaching for her arms delicately, to help lift her through the acts as Monty's eyes opened, looking at them.

"Just roll with it," she murmured to him with a little giggle, kissing his flesh once more. It was so much easier to fuck him in that position, without the hard ground beneath them, so she had no trouble riding his cock without help. She had to wonder how lazy the royals were to not even be able to do something so immensely enjoyable on their own.

But as she felt the sets of various hands on her flesh, lifting her up, guiding her, moving her at an exact match of the pace she'd set before, she could see a bit of the appeal. Two more had come in behind her, and their hands were on her arms, her waist, her thighs, until her father slid his hands up to her breasts. Freed of the need to help her ride his dick, he instead just put his hands to work fondling those breasts.

"Such perfect tits... made just for my enjoyment," he said with a grin, watching them jiggle with her motions up and down his thick, glistening cock.

"They're going to be monstrous once I'm pregnant," she said, looking down at her tits as they bounced. "I might have to be tied to the bed just to keep me from hurting my back trying to lug them around all day. Or maybe we could get someone to make a cute little under-bra..." she mused. A smirk formed on her lips as she thought, "With the tits still open of course. I wouldn't dream of denying you that."

Monty grinned at her, as her hands rested on his chest, and her body rose up and down, bouncing on his cock with such a delightful cadence to the rhythm of their rutting. The slap of their flesh together filling the room, his dick swelling and spurting pre into her as he shuddered and moaned.

"Damn right, it's tits out. I'll make it a law that these perfect tits never get hidden again from my eyes, if I must," he said with a cocky grin, his strong hands cupping, caressing, squeezing her breasts as he enjoyed everything about her, moaning and shivering.

"Perhaps just some little jewels to draw your eyes, should they ever start to wander," she grinned, watching his face as he fondled her tanned breasts. Her hips kept grinding against him, the hands of servants helping her keep her tempo in a surprisingly accurate way.

Any time she adjusted for speed, they took over and bore the brunt of it. All she had to do was the slightest of motions, and they were pumping her up and down her father's cock as hard as she liked. It was so very strange, but at the same time... she could get used to it.

"Mmm, I like the sound of that," Monty said, eying her breasts, imagining what they'd be like with some jewels. "A lovely little piercing... with a teardrop gemstones dangling from your nipple," he said, giving one of those sensitive little buds a flick of his finger.

It sent a jolt of pleasure through her and she moaned, a shiver traveling the length of her spine.

"I'm always eager for the Pharaoh to design me in his own image. Mould me into his perfect princess," she purred before correcting herself, "into his perfect Great Royal Wife. Isn't that what I said I wanted all along?" she asked, her breathing low and lusty against his earlobe.

"Fuck," he gasped out, feeling himself near his end. But then, as if summoned by his mind, one of the servant's caressed their dainty little hand on his balls, and gently tugged that package. He knew immediately what they were doing, and it worked. That gentle motion helped prolong his stamina, and he shivered as he spurt more pre-cum into his daughter.

"Maybe... maybe we should host a new Royal Wedding... to renew our vows for all to see," he said, licking his lower lip as he watched her tits bounce, her gorgeous body suspended by all those diligent hands holding her, moving her up and down his dick. "So that everyone knows how perfect the Pharaoh's daughter-wife is, as we lead them into a new era."

"I would love to be your bride once more," she said, her mouth quickly pressing against his. Excitement and lust vibrated through her and she clung to him so tightly as they made out. She was moaning on his tongue, her pussy tightening around his shaft, teasing them both as she got closer to her own finale.

"Then I will decree it so," he said, his breathing heavier, panting softly as she rode his dick with the aid of their many servants. "I'll inform them all of my intentions tomorrow. The grandest wedding of all time, for me..." he reached up, sliding his fingers along her cheek, caressing her face, "and the beautiful daughter I created to be my bride, forever."

Her gaze was on his again, the electricity between them sizzling as their bodies brought such pleasure to the both of them. She was losing control of her breath, little mewls of lust escaping from her lips every few seconds, but she refused to close her eyes. She wanted to see him as he came in her, and she wanted him to see her in turn.

As if the same thought were in both their heads, he stared into her eyes, caressed her face, and managed a few final words as his breathing grew heavier, and the servant released his heavy, cum-laden balls.

"Take it... receive the seed that made you, and provide for me my heir," he said with a mix of cockiness, playfulness, and deep seated love and devotion all in one. And he shuddered, moaned, and his whole body tensed up, his sculpted muscles bulging as he began to shoot off thick strands of his seed into his daughter's pussy.

The swelling of his cock, the way it thrust further into her, the knowledge of their forbidden lust... It all blended into something so intense that Leah's entire body just seemed to erupt. She had to fight to keep her eyes open, to watch him, but that just brought her to the next level of nirvana. As he came into her, she came on him, her pussy tightening around his cock, drawing every drop of his potent seed deeper into her womb.

And the servants helped as her father gripped her by the hips and shoved her down tight around his cock, keeping her pinned tightly against each other, locking every bit of seed inside her fertile depths as he shuddered and moaned, shooting off more and more of that rich cum. He could barely keep his own eyes open either, and the two of them gripped each other, trembling and moaning.

"It's... it's so perfectly... perfectly wrong trying to knock you up," he groaned out.

"I know, baby," she purred, kissing the corner of his lip, his cheek, before nuzzling into his ear. "But we've never wanted anything so bad in all our lives. So we might as well give in."

His eyes finally shut, and he nodded to her words, kissing her back, nuzzling against her as his dick swelled and shot off the last few spurts into her depths. He squeezed her, gripped her, held onto her like someone might take her away from him.

"I want the rest of our days to be like this," he said, panting.

"We will," she murmured into his ear. "We'll make this our life. You are the only man for me."

He was spent, and it was dark in the room, with the servants having lit braziers and candles all around for light. He'd fucked his daughter repeatedly that day, and still he felt he could go again, if his flesh weren't tired and weary from all the fighting and walking and rutting.

"You are the perfect girl for me," he rumbled, kissing her back, opening his eyes again to gaze at her longingly. "Help the Great Royal Wife to her bed chambers, without spilling a drop of my divine seed," he said, a wry smile on his face as the servants began to lift her up. A dainty hand cupping her mound so carefully, with such practice, that as his dick slipped out of her, nothing had a chance to spill.

It was such a strange sensation, but truthfully, Leah was okay with it, so long as it meant that she kept his seed within her. She relaxed back, swallowing back another whimpered moan, allowing the servants to bring her to the room.

It was lewd and elegant all at once, the way they carried her--and thereby guided him--to their bedroom. A large place, with a canopy bed adorned with endless arrays of silk cushions. And there the two of them lay down to rest, unaware of the many schemes going on around them in the court of the Sun King.

But as Monty put his arm around Leah, held her close,

they felt utter contentment in that moment. And as Monty's large, strong hand drifted down over her tummy, he felt the truth: that his seed had taken root, and his child was growing inside of her.

Subscribe for more Candy Quinn:
http://candyquinn.com/newsletter

Recommended For You

For a full list of all my books, or to browse by length or kink, please visit my website!

https://candyquinn.com/books

YOUR NEXT HOT READ

Seducing the Hawthornes

Shipwrecked Brat

Stranded Beauty

Free Exclusive Story

LUST LESSONS: BELLA

She has the hots for teacher

Mr. Wright is totally off limits. Not only is he her teacher, but he's also her brother's best friend.

Bella has never wanted anyone more. At first, she just

wants to tease him. She doesn't wear panties, and practically begs him for the big D —- detention — just to prove to him how good she is at being bad. But he wants more than a tease. He wants to claim her fertile, innocent body, and neither of them can resist their forbidden desires.

TEASER

By the time the bell rang and the other students rushed out, Bella's fantasies had her wound up tighter than a knot. Her bare pussy was dripping on her chair, and she slipped out of it eagerly.

"Well, Mr. Wright, you got me alone," she grinned.

Clark gave her a cautionary look, before he went to the door and shut it tight then locked it.

"You really chose an... interesting way to get yourself in trouble, Bella," he said to her as he returned from the door, shaking his head at her in surprised disbelief, a soft chuckle escaping his lips. "But you always were a little terror of a tease," he said as he made his way back towards the class windows, beginning to slide the curtains shut.

"You make it sound so sweet," she giggled, sitting on his desk. She pulled her white skirt out from under her, crossing her legs as she watched him shut the curtains. "I just did what felt natural."

Get your free copy of Lust Lessons: Bella, and so much more! All you have to do is subscribe to my newsletter.
http://candyquinn.com/newsletter

Become Candy Obsessed

For over a decade, I've been writing the hottest, naughtiest stories I can think of, and I'm addicted. I love to explore the forbidden, the taboo, and the over-the-top sexy. Each story starts off with a sizzle, giving you that nice build up, and that perfect release.

Discover new, secret fantasies, or just indulge in those sticky-sweet guilty pleasures. I'll never judge! Make sure to follow me on your fave site so you never miss a new release.

Plus, if you **sign up for my mailing list**, you'll get updates on my new books, bundles, giveaways, and several **free, exclusive books.**

CONNECT WITH CANDY!
candyquinn.com
candyquinn.com/newsletter
candy.quinn.erotica@gmail.com

FOLLOW ME EVERYWHERE!

f facebook.com/candyquinnromance

y twitter.com/sexycandyquinn

a amazon.com/Candy-Quinn/e/B00K187NCE

BB bookbub.com/authors/candy-quinn

Also by Candy Quinn

NOVELS

Stranded Princess

Seducing the Hawthornes

Campus Cravings

NOVELLAS

Taboo Passions Layla & Landon

Shipwrecked Brat

Stranded Beauty

Innocent Farm Girl

Precious Pet

The Fugitive

Dirty Country Love

Sylvia & Zach Collection

Protector

Mandy Collection

Nympho Farm Girl

Biker's Sugar Babe Nympho Pet

Claimed by the Bad Boy Biker

Innocent Tease

The Delaney Brothers

Alastair

Jack

Tristan

William

SERIES

Campus Stud

Campus Stud 1: The Hottie Prof Takes His V

Campus Stud 2: The Wet Cheerleader in the Lockers

Campus Stud 3: The Fertile Professor Begs for His Seed

Campus Stud 4: The Goth Chick First Time Rear

Campus Stud 5: The Little Thief Fertile First Time

Naughty Nympho

#1: Stretched and Filled for the First Time

#2: Addicted to His Cream

#3: Obsessed with His D

#4: Cuckqueened by His Ex

#5: Desperate to be Stretched and Taken

#6: Hotwife for Money

Nympho Babe

Nympho Amber

Nympho Halloween

Nympho Angel

Nympho Off the Pill

Nympho for the Gang

Nympho Valentine

TABOO STEP-DADDY

HIS BRAT'S FERTILE FIRST TIME

Avril

Blaire

Cassidy

Delilah

Raina

Taboo Temptress

Taking the Fertile Brat

The Billionaire and the Brat

Teaching the Brat

The Priest's Brat

Pregnant Brat for Christmas

Cam Girl for the Man of the House

Bratty Chrissy

Honey Trapping the Man of the House

Seducing the Man of the House

Spoiled Brat

Rich Brat

Summer Heat

Flirting with the Man of the House

Her Forbidden Cherry

Love Spell

TABOO STEP-BROTHER/SISTER

Taboo Passions Layla & Landon

Stepbrother's Baby

Valley Girl Tease

Unleashed Fantasies

Taboo Passions Lilly & Leo 1

Taboo Passions Lilly & Leo 2

Taboo Passions Lilly & Leo 3

Taboo Passions Aeris & Aiden 1

Taboo Passions Aeris & Aiden 2

Taboo Passions Emma & Brody

Taboo Passions Bella and Colton

Taboo Christmas Micah and Sage

Taboo Christmas Nadine and Andy

Taboo Christmas Parker and Kinsley

Taboo Threesome

Sylvia & Zach 1

Sylvia & Zach 2

VIRGIN BREEDING

BREEDING

BDSM

Fertile Freshman for the Team

SUGAR DADDIES

Sugar Baby Paige

Christine's Sugar Daddies

Karen's Sugar Daddy

Olivia's Sugar Daddy

Sugar Daddy Rock Star

Sugar Daddy Camgirl

Sugar Daddy Influencer

Sugar Daddy Student

THE FERTILE FARM

The Fertile Farm Olive

Nympho Farm Girl

Mandy Collection

The Fertile Farm Rosa

The Fertile Farm Lucy

The Fertile Farm Daisy

The Fertile Farm Dixie

Fertile Farm Laura's Innocence 1

Fertile Farm Laura's Innocence 2

The Farmgirl & The Fugitive

The Farmgirl & The Bandit

The Military Man & Farmgirl

Bought by the Billionaire

MFM BREEDING

Her Fertile First Time

Her Fertile Second Time

BECCA, KATIE & LYNN

Fertile First Time Becca

Fertile First Time Katie

Fertile First Time Lynn

SHARING HER

Buying Her

Catering to Her

Exhibitionist for Her

Teaching Her

Rocking Her

Trading for Her

Stealing Her

Awakening Her

Punishing Her

Blindfolding Her

BUNDLES

Forbidden Temptations

Fertile Farmgirl Collection

Fertile Farms

First Taste of Candy

Taboo Brats

Tasting Candy

First Times

Candy Quinn's Dirty Fantasies

Lickable Candy Bundle

Sharing Her Bundle

Three Fertile First Times

Fertile First Time with the Gang